THE CLOTHES
IN THE WARDROBE

Alice Thomas Ellis

PENGUIN BOOKS

PENGUIN BOOKS

Published by the Penguin Group
27 Wrights Lane, London W8 5TZ, England
Viking Penguin Inc., 40 West 23rd Street, New York, New York 10010, USA
Penguin Books Australia Ltd, Ringwood, Victoria, Australia
Penguin Books Canada Ltd, 2801 John Street, Markham, Ontario, Canada L3R 1B4
Penguin Books (NZ) Ltd, 182–190 Wairau Road, Auckland 10, New Zealand

Penguin Books Ltd, Registered Offices: Harmondsworth, Middlesex, England

First published by Gerald Duckworth & Co. Ltd 1987
Published in Penguin Books 1989
1 3 5 7 9 10 8 6 4 2

Printed and bound in Great Britain by
Cox & Wyman Ltd, Reading
Photoset in North Wales by
Derek Doyle & Associates, Mold, Clwyd

I remembered her all my life. For years the image of her had hung in my mind like a portrait in a high room, seldom observed but unchanging. Sometimes, unawares, I would see her again suddenly revealed in the vaulting halls of my head. She was sitting on a grassy bank, leaning forward a little, a cigarette between her fingers, and she was speaking. I could not remember what she was saying, nor even if I had understood her, but I knew that what she was saying must be, in some sense, significant. She wore a cream-coloured cotton frock with large puffed sleeves, sprigged with tiny brown flowers; her stockings were cream-coloured too and on her feet were white, barred shoes. Her hair grew in dry red curls, dark red like rust or winter bracken. She was not at all beautiful, but even with her likeness before me I had always assumed that she must be, since she carried such conviction in her forgotten words and her enduring appearance. Her name was Lili.

*

'Margaret,' called my mother, and 'Margaret' again, her voice taking on the faint exasperation that had flavoured her tone as she used my name for many years now. I sometimes wondered whether she had been angry with the infant Margaret and whether I had feared her always.

'The guest list,' she said, standing in the hall before the looking-glass, removing her hat and jabbing stiff-fingered at her hair. 'Have you thought about the guest list?'

I stood in the doorway of the sitting-room and said that I had.

'Invitations,' said my mother. 'I must send out the invitations.'

She came into the sitting-room and sniffed. 'I wish you'd eat in the kitchen or the dining-room,' she complained.

I had eaten an orange and thrown the peel on the fire just as I lit it, and the smell of orange zest and smoke embittered the air while the peel lay, mock flame, amid the cold coals.

'If you'd chosen to be married in June,' remarked my mother, doubtless moved by the aroma to an association of ideas, 'the mock-orange blossom would have been out.'

I thought that I hadn't chosen to get married at all but that Syl had chosen to marry me, since it was time for him to marry and I offered no threat to the way and integrity of his life and character, and that my mother had chosen to see me wed because I was good for little else.

'On the other hand,' added my mother hastily, as though she feared that I might take the chance to postpone the ceremony in order to accommodate the philadelphus, 'chrysanthemums are more reliable. They don't wilt so quickly, and those dark red ones are really very attractive against the grey stone.'

I told my mother with timid spite, hidden terror and a certain mad braggadoccio that in some countries chrysanthemums were considered appropriate only for funerals.

'This is not some countries,' retorted my mother, perhaps wondering again whether the money she had spent so that I might learn French and a little grace had been utterly wasted, for I had learned only superstition and discontent.

'For goodness sake go and put some lipstick on,' she said. 'If Syl comes he'll think you're dying.'

6

I was too meek to tell her that I wished I was. Nor would it have been true, for I greatly feared death, suspecting myself to be damned.

My mother glanced at the clock before looking at the window to ascertain that the garden was already retreating into night, and drew the curtains.

'I don't suppose you've written down the guests you want to ask?' she remarked.

' I've got a list somewhere,' I said.

My mother, quite properly, did not believe me, but as I was now clearly an adult, even if an unsatisfactory one, she could not directly accuse me of lying. Frustrated, she went towards the kitchen and I pulled the curtains apart to watch night fall.

*

'It doesn't fit,' I said with satisfaction.

My mother couldn't deny it. The wedding dress hung loosely on me and I appeared to myself, reflected in the cheval mirror, gratifyingly ridiculous.

'It looks silly,' I said more positively.

My mother irritatedly seized two handfuls of the old brocade and dragged them behind my back.

'You've lost weight,' she observed in a tone which indicated that she could have expected nothing else of me. 'It'll have to be taken in at the seams.'

Already the tiny triumph had withered in me. I thought the dead whiteness of the dress made me more of a corpse than a bride but hadn't enough energy to infuriate my mother by telling her so.

'For goodness sake liven up,' she said. 'Syl will think he's going to a funeral not a wedding.'

This was not percipience in my mother, but a belated

7

riposte to my revelation, the day before, of the role of the chrysanthemum in foreign culture.

'I've never known such a miserable bride,' she went on, standing back and looking at me with some affection, but more disapproval. 'What's the matter with you?'

This was the first time she had admitted openly that all was not well; and I was forced to reassure her, for otherwise she might find herself in sympathy with me, she might come to my side, and this was unthinkable, for to be understood by her was a prospect beyond endurance.

'I am only cold,' I said. 'It is cold after Egypt.' And dark, I thought. Dark, dark.

My mother wasn't one for silences. As she pulled the dress over my head she said that she thought it would still fit *her*, that she could see the hole at the neckline where my grandmother had pinned a pearl brooch as something old, that the classic line never dated. Moved by an ancient sentiment as she cradled the dress, so that it lolled in her arms like someone drowned, she said that she was glad she had a daughter to wear it; and I said, politely, that I could see it must be a pleasing economy.

My mother couldn't refute this without venturing further into sentiment, and this she would not do.

'I had a letter from Lili this morning,' she said. 'They're back in England.'

I was silent, for the news meant nothing to me.

'She saw the announcement in *The Times*,' continued my mother.

As I was still silent she went on, 'You must remember Lili. She was my bridesmaid.'

'I don't remember her,' I said, but I lied. I remembered her now. It was a small shock to know that the neglected image in my mind was real, that she lived and breathed, read *The Times* and wrote letters to her old friends.

8

'I shall ask her to stay for the wedding,' said my mother. 'Her and Robert.'

Suddenly I remembered Robert too. A man behind Lili. A bearded, shapeless man in brown and purple woollens. A painter.

'He's an artist,' said my mother. 'It's years since I've seen them. They stayed in Egypt. Lili's father was tremendously rich until the government sequestered all his property. If I'd thought, you could have stayed with them, but I don't suppose you'd have learned much French.'

I hadn't. I had learned very little, but my mother had no means of testing me. I had learned other things.

*

In those days I slept a great deal, and sometimes I dreamed: not of what had happened but of emptiness and occasionally of chaos when the tenuous mosaic that was life shattered into its constituent parts and whirled away into unknown infinities. I would wake sleep-logged and weary, and every new day was dull. After a while it seemed to me amusing that such preparations as a wedding involve should surround the plain, pale husk that was me and that no one had commented on this incongruity. Even my mother had closed her eyes and ceased to speak of bridal nerves, and my groom, who meant as little to me as his mother's dog, was just as he had always been.

I was trapped, not only by the ordering of the caterers, the priest and my mother's new hat, but by an impotence of spirit. Sometimes in the evenings I would hear myself laughing, and the sound was like wind passing over an empty vessel. One day I overheard my mother speaking to a friend, or rather to an acquaintance, since she was clearly deemed worthy only of instant or cliché speech. My mother said casually, 'Oh, the honeymoon will soon put the roses back in her cheeks.' And for a moment despair was overwhelmed by something more lively: by a sensation of such disgust that for just that one moment I was almost galvanized into rebellion. My mother had intended no lewdness, but the connotations of her remark had made me feel a greater, more immediate sense of defilement than that which I already experienced. Then I shut my mind to the picture that her words had conjured, for after all – what did it matter? My mother had lived my life until half a year ago when I had so briefly lived my own and in the process destroyed it. Now I was to be given to Syl. I had nothing to lose. For Syl I felt no sympathy, since if he was fool enough to want me he deserved none. In the course of time I would die and then it would all be over.

We went to the theatre and to dinner and I believe I must have talked and, as I have said, I know I sometimes laughed and I think no one ever knew that I was empty of everything except perhaps madness.

I spent as little time with Syl as I possibly could. He didn't seem to mind. He had few friends but many acquaintances. He played tennis and golf and sometimes went swimming, determined to give no appearance of succumbing to time, to age. I saw that he could not marry a woman of his own generation, for that would double his chances of seeming old. It was sad for me, I thought, that I was the only girl in the world sufficiently stupid to permit herself to be sacrificed to his vanity. I had few friends, just one or two left over from school, but on the infrequent occasions when we met I could see from their faces that they pitied me, finding me foolish and Syl a bore. He somehow seemed familiar with the jokes that the young were making and used their slang. He embarrassed my friends, and I saw them less and less. He even behaved to

10

my mother, his exact contemporary, as though she were much older than he, deferring to her opinions with an air of youthful naiveté. She colluded with him. I had seen her ruffle his hair as though he were a little boy. I knew myself to be stupid, but I sometimes felt that I wasn't alone, and that stupidity was a condition which age did not ease. This was against all that was implicit in the way I had been taught – people increased in wisdom as they grew older, so that they were able to guide the young in the paths they should follow. But my mother had no learning, no wide experience: merely the prejudices, the powerfully surviving clichés, of her own upbringing. Knowing this, I was still impotent, for I had nothing to put in its stead, no one to turn to for advice or support, and I had learned for myself nothing of life except that I was bad at living, and that where I loved I met only rejection and disaster. My father feared my mother as much as I did and wished me to please and agree with her always, for when I did not she would complain to him of my behaviour and I suspected that when this happened his new wife would complain in her turn that he paid too much attention to us and too little to her and her own children. I didn't like to cause trouble. Trouble-makers were visible by reason of their demeanour and I wished to be observed as little as possible. I wished to get through life along the lanes and side roads, unseen.

*

One weekend I went with Syl to stay with some people in the country. I don't remember much about it, only dim rooms and fire-light, a dinner of steak-and-kidney pudding and broccoli, which I recall because I disliked it – the smell of urine in the meat, laughter at conversation I did not understand.

11

There was a boy there of my own age and we got drunk together at the far end of a room with a bottle of martini. He put his head on my shoulder and undid the buttons of my blouse. As fast as he undid them I did them up again, so that when he got to my waist and sighed he recoiled with indignation and astonishment to find that his labour had been in vain. I was too drunk to wonder whether we had been observed and too remote to care. I had no fear of him and was pleased with my own ingenuity.

My head spun that night, and all next day I felt weak and disordered. The boy in the daylight reminded me of a bird, a bold curious bird. He asked me questions about Syl and about myself without any pretence at politeness. I felt even more fearful than usual faced with this clever inquisitive boy who showed no further desire to undo my blouse and who was only interested in the incongruity of my relationship with Syl. I wanted to tell him calmly that I knew perfectly well that it was absurd and quite understood the point of his questions. Clever as he was, he wasn't sufficiently clever to see this, and his assumption that I was half-witted made me stubbornly worse.

Syl was away all day with our host, shooting something, and I was too shy to say I was tired and would like to go and sleep in my room. I spent hours with that wretched boy evading his questions and seeming more stupid by the minute. I never did discover who he was, the son of the house or just another guest, and my own obtuseness and incuriosity now appear to me more revealing than anything else of my state at the time. Healthy creatures do not behave so in strange surroundings.

Our hostess scarcely showed herself at all. I suppose she was in the kitchen, perhaps avoiding me, and perhaps the boy had been instructed to entertain me. I didn't wonder about it then. I was no more alert to my environment than a sick animal and I must have somehow been aware of that, because it was then that I remembered the starveling cat.

When we got home my mother asked if we had had a good time and Syl said with great enthusiasm that we had.

Perhaps he had. I never knew him.

*

When Lili came to stay the emphasis shifted slightly, away from me and on to the strange woman.

She hadn't altered. Her clothes were different – foreign, and smart – but her hair was red, and although I could see she wasn't beautiful I thought she was. She had such colour, such brightness, that sometimes she reminded me of the whirling mosaics, except that she wasn't fragmented but unusually complete. She seemed, if anything, younger than I remembered her. Only one thing surprised me – I didn't recognise her voice and I had thought I would.

She said as she entered, 'My dears ...' in a very English fashion, and she said all the usual phrases, and then to me, 'I hope you're doing the right thing.'

'Now then, Lili,' said my mother.

'You must just forget I'm here,' said Lili. 'You must go on with the preparations as though you were alone. I promise I won't even offer to help. I shan't get in the way for a moment.'

'Where's Robert?' enquired my mother accusingly. 'I thought Robert was coming with you.'

'Oh, he *is*,' said Lili. 'Robert always comes with me. He had to see a man about a gallery.'

'Will he be here for dinner?' asked my mother, the cook briefly taking precedence over the hostess.

'I shouldn't think so,' said Lili. 'I shouldn't think so for a moment.' She moved to the foot of the stairs. 'Am I in the

13

same room?' she asked.

'Yes, Lili,' said my mother.

I thought she sounded rather as though she too had forgotten the essence of Lili, was now reminded and was regretting her invitation.

'Margaret will help you up with your bags.'

Lili glanced at me. 'You look quite strong,' she said, picking up the largest of the suitcases and dragging it up the stairs. 'I remember the smell of this house. I remember you when you were little.'

In the bedroom she turned to me, 'You look tired,' she observed. 'Aren't you sleeping?'

'I sleep too much,' I said, startled into the truth.

'It sometimes takes one that way,' she said obscurely, hunting through her handbag for her cigarettes and lighter.

My stomach tightened. My mother took a firm line on smoking in bedrooms.

Lili lit her cigarette and looked in the mirror.

'Hag,' she addressed herself.

*

'I'd forgotten how loud and exhausting she could be,' remarked my mother later as I peeled the potatoes.

I looked nervously at her face, but it wore a smile, a reminiscent smile that I hadn't seen before.

'She was expelled from school,' said my mother. 'But I never thought she was really bad – just mischievous and high-spirited.'

It came to me that my mother was *proud* of her friendship with this high-spirited outcast, and I felt resentment as I thought of my own upbringing, of the fuss when my school reports weren't all that my mother would have wished, of the scene when once I had sworn. My mother is a hypocrite, I thought incredulously. Then I forgot about it as the carrots boiled over. But already Lili had added a new dimension to my view.

*

'And how is Syl?' asked Lili over dinner.

This too, astounded me. Syl was more of my mother's generation than my own but it had never occurred to me before that he and she and Lili must all have been young at the same time. I realised that until recently I had thought very little, had taken life at face value, as though, until I was born, nothing on the earth had moved.

My mother, it seemed to me, looked shifty. She said, 'Syl's fine.' She added, 'He's very good to Margaret', and I felt that simultaneously she had nodded towards the past while affirming the present and that I had fallen somewhere between the two: nothing but the body of a ghost, nebulous and deserted.

'Is he still as good-looking?' asked Lili.

Again I was astonished, for Syl was hard and red and, as I had just realised, old.

'It seems like forever since we were last here. Hasn't he changed at all?'

Lili looked sideways at me and then away. I thought it the gesture of someone who has noticed a fellow human being about to step in something horrible but who is too polite to draw attention to the fact by seeming sorry for her. I didn't yet know Lili.

'He plays games,' said my mother. 'Keeps himself in trim.'

'Hmm,' said Lili, mashing a carrot.

'Prime of life,' said my mother, sounding to my ears defensive.

'But of course,' said Lili. 'Aren't we all?'

Not I, I thought. And not you, Mother.

Then Lili laughed and seemed to gleam with deathlessness and, I thought, the pride of life. Then I remembered, the lust of the eyes and the lust of the flesh, and thought of the quiet convent and cool water.

'Egypt,' my mother was saying; 'tell Lili what you thought of Egypt.'

I said, 'It was very nice.'

Lili laughed again. 'She has the right instincts,' she said. 'She is too polite to bore us with a travelogue.'

She lit a cigarette and asked what I had thought of Marie Claire.

I said I had found her very kind.

'She was always kind at school,' said Lili. 'She used to share her sweets, but I never thought she had the sense of a hen.'

'She was cleverer than all of us,' protested my mother. 'Top of the class.'

'I'm not talking about cleverness,' said Lili, 'I said *sense*.'

My mother said she thought the two qualities went together and Lili said they didn't: not necessarily, and in many cases they were mutually exclusive. My mother couldn't understand this and accused Lili of talking drivel.

Unwisely, I spoke. I felt relief that someone who had known Marie Claire for so long should share my opinion of her. 'She was *daft*,' I said.

'You are in no position, Margaret,' said my mother, 'to judge Marie Claire.'

I knew she was angry because this appraisal reflected badly on her judgement. She could hardly bear to be contradicted, and no good mother, in my mother's view, would send her child to stay with a daft person.

I think it was now that Lili decided I stood in need of

care. As she went on talking, making occasional references to the length of my fingers or the breadth of my brow, I thought it ironical that this odd woman should be defending me, not from outright attack but from my mother's protectiveness. I felt like the babes in the wood concealed by leaves lovingly given. I consoled myself; for if it is not possible to be free, perhaps to be hidden is the next best thing, and Lili's presence gave me, as the hours went by, the feeling that I was growing less visible. I was scarcely called upon to say a word as she talked, pale smoke drifting from her mouth and her nose and hanging in the light.

*

Just before bedtime Lili reverted again to the topic of my marriage.

'And will Derek be coming?' she asked. Derek was my father.

'Yes,' said my mother looking consciously civilised. She had been outraged when her husband left for another woman, had addressed him with religious vehemence and spoken of hell, but as time passed she had realised that life was very much more pleasant without him, that he was generous with money, and so she had, not forgiven, but ceased to revile him; and I know she found grim amusement in my stepmother's harrassed countenance and the irritating ways of her two small children. They would come sometimes for my birthday, or at Christmas, and my mother, whose material circumstances were very much more comfortable than those of my father and his new family, would patronise them and condole with my stepmother on my father's drinking habits and the undisciplined weeping of her little boy. The girl bade fair to be pretty but fortunately was extremely dim.

17

'He'll be here with his family,' said my mother. 'The children are going to be page and bridesmaid.' She wore a momentary look of almost angelic forbearance. 'I was doubtful when I first had the idea, but Margaret has no cousins or ...' Here she bit a potato, because she had been going to say 'close friends' but had thought better of it. She had lost her temper with me on the subject of bridesmaids. Of course there were friends whom I could have asked, but I had seen an opportunity to be stubborn and had dismissed each of her suggested candidates with tiresome and irrelevant objections – too fat, too blonde, too tall, too many teeth. 'Then we'll have Jennifer and Christopher,' my mother had said in a barely controlled fury. 'All right,' I had said listlessly, disconcerting my mother considerably, since I was perfectly aware that she had expected me to turn down this preposterous proposal with as much intractability as I had turned down the others. She was now determined at least to win admiration for her enforced magnanimity.

'What's his wife like?' asked Lili.

'She's a nice little thing,' said my mother damningly.

Lili, who I could tell understood her very well, laughed and lit another cigarette.

'She's called Cynthia,' said my mother as one who says, 'She's called cat-sick.'

'Ugh,' said Lili obligingly.

*

There was a small summer-house at the bottom of my mother's garden, half wood, half glass. I used to, as my mother put it, 'curl up with a book' on a broad shelf which ran the length of one wall under shaky moorish windows which looked out over the golf course. On the opposite shelf

18

stood my mother's collection of cactuses. She refused to have any pets in the house, but even the hardest of hearts need some discharge of sentiment. This usually presents as sentimentality and my mother talked to her cactuses with affection and called them sweet names. I very much resented them, because they drew my mother to what would have been a private retreat for me. Most days she would, sooner or later, walk down the lawn to examine her plants and I learned to wait until she had done this before myself settling in the summer-house. Once I waited so long and stayed so late that I gave myself away to Syl, who had called in the usual way at the front door, to be told by my mother that I was in the summer-house and he should go and bring me out and back to the drawing-room where, like normal people, we should converse. After that Syl took to walking from his garden along the edge of the golf course to my mother's garden. He would look in the summer-house before coming in by the back door but he seldom found me there now.

'If you want to do something useful,' my mother said to me one day, 'you can help me propagate the cactuses.'

When bits of them broke off you had only to plunge them into the earth and they grew into new cactuses. I didn't want to do anything useful. There were very few human beings I cared for and I cared nothing for cactuses.

'You're very selfish,' my mother said. 'If you took more of an interest in things you'd be happier.'

I knew I was selfish. I knew that people who loved God were supposed to love their neighbour too. But Syl was our neighbour.

I said I'd go shopping for her instead, and she said that that was unnecessary since Mrs Raffald had already done it. I said I'd tear out the dead michaelmas daisies, but the gardener had done that. There was really very little I could

19

do actively to refute the charge of selfishness. Even the local cats were, without exception, well-fed and cared for, and there wasn't a needy creature for miles round. In order to express charity and compassion I would have to travel far, since nobody near would have thanked me for it.

'When you're married you'll have to be less selfish,' said my mother, who was particularly displeased with me on this grey, wintry morning. 'You'll have to brighten up.'

I was disposed to argue. 'Why?' I asked.

'Syl won't put up with all this nonsense,' said my mother unwarily.

'I'd better break the engagement now,' I said, thinking my mother very foolish for not realising that what appealed to Syl was my very paleness, my silence, my hostility, which he mostly construed as shyness, until I was unpleasant, and when I was unpleasant he took it as evidence of some depth in my feeling for him and found it sexually alluring. I had once or twice been goaded by his obtuseness into cruelty and he had wanted me more. I had been brought close to another sort of despair by my inability to draw blood: a cat with no claws and ineffectual teeth. Such a cat can seem only like a toy.

'You can't break the engagement now,' said my mother.

'Why?' I asked.

'You know perfectly well,' said my mother, not going into details.

In a sane world, I thought, we would have discussed the state of my feelings, debated whether I loved Syl sufficiently to commit the rest of my life to him, questioned my views on the institution of marriage, examined my mother's motives in striving to introduce me into this state, have said *something* of some interest. But the cake had been ordered and that was that. There was no more to be said.

*

20

I was ill at ease in the mornings in those days. I would wake sour-mouthed, unwilling to get out of bed. My mother would bring me China tea and toast, succulent with butter, and I would eat it, knowing that afterwards I should feel sick and heavy. I would remember, against my will, the fragrance of coffee and hot bread, the energy that had possessed me so short a time ago, when I had felt supple as an eel, as powerful as a salmon, as sure and quiet and graceful as an owl. I would remember the sunlight that I had thought was like wealth, redeemed and transformed beyond the reach of cupidity, and the shadows that were not black but the colour of great half-forgotten riches. My own country now seemed mean and meretricious, and my feet clashed awkwardly with the ground, jarring my body and jangling my bones so that the sound of my clumsy movements echoed hollowly against thin walls, and I was never at peace. So short a time ago? It seemed like aeons of time ago in an unimaginably distant world. My childhood felt nearer. The useless girl that I was might have grown without diversion, etiolated and bland like a stalk of grass under a stone, from those early days, represented still by the dolls and bears that lay on the cupboard shelves. The living creature that I had briefly been might never have existed. My mother would not have recognised her, and now I scarcely recognised her myself.

I was so cold.

'I'm only spoiling you like this,' lied my mother, 'because when you've got a home of your own you won't have time for breakfast in bed.'

I sat up so that she could put the tray on my knees. She brought me breakfast in bed to ensure that I was awake and wouldn't spend the morning half-sleeping in frowsty tumbled sheets.

I said, like the child who had played with the dolls and

21

bears, 'Syl would bring me breakfast in bed, only his mother wouldn't let him.'

'I certainly hope you wouldn't expect him to,' said my mother. 'Syl is a busy man. No time to make breakfast for a lazy wife.'

She picked up my underclothes from the floor and laid them on a chair. 'I just wish you'd pull yourself together,' she said half despairingly.

But I knew what was really worrying her at that moment. It was the mention of Syl's mother who lived in his house and showed no intention, although she was nearly eighty, of ever dying. My mother frequently enquired after her health and was constantly disappointed. 'She's wonderful,' Syl would say, 'got the heart of a sixty-year-old.' He seemed not to dislike her, which was odd since apart from him all who knew her were united in this emotion.

'You'll hardly have to see her at all,' said my mother, voicing her worry tangentially, 'in a house that size.'

'We'll have to eat together,' I said in a doleful tone which I knew would upset my mother as much as the vision which my remark would conjure up. These petty revenges were my only source of pleasure, pallid though it was.

'Of course you won't,' said my mother, almost squeaking with exasperation. 'Why on earth do you think Syl went to all the trouble of making her a separate kitchen?'

Syl had indeed done this. He had taken the pleasantest, south-facing rooms of the house and turned them into what he described as a 'suite' for his parent.

'I could hardly expect her to eat alone,' I said. 'Poor old lady ...'

But I had gone too far. My mother glared at me suspiciously and told me not be so ridiculous.

Already the satisfaction of teasing her had faded. While I spoke like that I could pretend that Syl and his house were

22

unreal and my projected presence in it merely an extension of that fantasy, but the wedding loomed ever closer like a rock and I, poor ship, was about to founder on it. I had had a sudden image of Syl bringing me breakfast in a bed which we had shared, and I heard myself saying aloud, 'No!'

My mother who had reached the door turned to look at me.

'What?' she said.

'Nothing,' I said. 'I just thought of something. It wasn't anything.'

My mother was the sort of person who regards talking to yourself as the first sign of madness.

'What you need is a couple of babies,' she observed. 'That'll give you something to think about.'

I did so wish that my mother hadn't said that.

*

'How's the bride?' asked Lili when I came downstairs.

For some reason I didn't mind Lili talking about my wedding. I think I knew already that she didn't take it seriously.

'I'm dying to see Syl again. When is he coming?' She looked at her watch. 'Robert should be here soon.'

'Syl will come this evening,' I told her.

'Goody, we can have a party. It might cheer you up. On the other hand,' she added, 'it might not. I often find parties depressing. All that yelling and drinking and getting too hot. Parties have been known to make my make-up run. That's annoying.'

I found her calm assumption that I needed cheering up restful after my mother's blind denials.

'It isn't any fun being young,' said Lili. 'But people forget. I don't. I clearly remember it being detestable –

23

one's hormones haven't yet learned their place and one is full of uncertainties.'

My mother came in, flustered.

'I'm short of a chop,' she said. 'I just looked in the larder and I've only got four. Now if Syl stays to dinner we'll be five ...'

'I'll go and buy you one,' said Lili. 'I'll buy you half a dozen if you like. It isn't like you to fuss about a missing chop.'

'I've got so much on my mind,' said my mother irritably, letting us know that she was bearing the full burden of the forthcoming taxing ceremony.

'Me and Margaret will go,' said Lili. 'It'll be a nice little outing for us.'

My mother looked less harrassed.

'Margaret could do with some exercise,' she said. 'She hardly leaves the house. No wonder she's so pale.'

'Exercise is good for you,' said Lili as we walked, 'but I hate it. I can't see the point in going for a walk unless a chop lies at the end of it.'

'I used to walk in Egypt,' I said. Egypt.

I could sense Lili turning her head to look at me, but the urge to talk, to confess, had left me as suddenly as it had come.

'How did Syl propose?' asked Lili. 'Did he go down on one knee, hand on heart?'

I considered. What had happened was that Syl had, one evening, flushed with wine, remarked that he thought it would be a good idea if we got married. I had said nothing and he had assumed that we were engaged, telling his mother that night and mine the following morning. He had moved to kiss my mouth, but I had turned my head and he had kissed my cheek. Incomprehensible as it may seem, he and I had never shared an embrace. He had made many

24

attempts to put his arms around me, but I had always evaded him. As I thought about it it seemed extraordinary that any man should endure such behaviour and still wish to marry the object of his desire. Sometimes, he would whisper that I was an innocent little thing, a primrose, a little white pony and other endearments: strange, understated fantasies that I could not comprehend.

'He asked me to marry him,' I said at last, 'so I said I would.'

'Why?' asked Lili.

'I don't know,' I said, because of course I hadn't agreed at all. Simply I had known that I couldn't go on living with my mother. I had nowhere else to go and now I was being carried along – that ship bound for wrecking.

'I wonder if he's queer,' mused Lili aloud. 'I always used to wonder if he might be. And now he's forty, unmarried and still living with that old termagant he calls Mother.'

'He's had girl friends,' I protested, just to be fair.

'I know that,' said Lili, 'but he was always a bit strange with them. Too *helpful*, if you see what I mean.'

I did. Syl would have liked to take my shoes off for me, brush my hair, and once he had muttered that he would gladly wash my clothes.

'Tell you what I think,' said Lili cheerfully. 'He's either a masochist or, in view of your age, a paedophile.'

I thought that this was a most extraordinary conversation to be having about one's intended groom, but I was feeling lighter. Lili, I thought, would be ruthless with cobwebs, dauntless in darkened rooms, relentless with dust accumulated in hidden corners. I wanted her to go on talking, but she lost interest, turned into the butcher's and struck up a conversation about meat.

This was the first time I had seen her exercise her charm. After two minutes I believe the butcher would have followed her out of the shop had she beckoned him. With talk of sweetbreads and liver and fillet she captivated him – I couldn't quite see how she did it. She would look at him sideways, smile at unexpected moments, and while she was never coarse there was the vaguest suggestion of the gentlest possible obscenity as she spoke of the bodies of animals. However, she did it well, and I shouldn't think the butcher ever quite forgot the lady with the red hair.

I felt inclined to congratulate her on her performance as we left with our solitary chop, but her interest had turned again and she was speaking of Egypt. I tensed myself, but Lili's Egypt wasn't mine. She spoke of painting and antiquities while I thought of rivers, dark faces and the shadowed cloisters of the convent.

We stopped again to buy olive oil and garlic, for Lili said that although she had vowed not to interfere she was going to cook dinner and, while my mother would complain, she would be grateful in the end.

'I shall cook an Egyptian meal,' said Lili.

She put her arm around me briefly.

'Make you feel at home,' she added.

I wondered if she could see into my mind, and I didn't care, for during that one short walk I had come to believe that Lili would not harm me.

*

Robert, unlike Lili, had changed considerably. He wasn't the bulky, bearded man of my memory but thin, clean-shaven, dark and angry.

'Do stop worrying,' Lili ordered him, after he had spent some time fulminating against the iniquities of the gallery owner. 'It'll be all right on the night.'

'You haven't seen the lighting,' he said.

26

'We'll make the man change it,' promised Lili. 'You mustn't bore the bride's mother with art-world horror stories. She has enough to think about.'

Robert then spoke to my mother about the time when they were young. He only mentioned the gallery once more when Syl arrived, clapped him on the shoulder and asked him what he was up to now.

'Syl,' said Lili coolly, as he turned to her, 'how nice to see you. You've hardly changed at all.'

I said without thinking, 'I wonder what you were all like when you were young?', realising as I spoke how young I was myself as four people in early middle age turned to regard me with varying degrees of indignation and amusement.

I do wish you'd make some effort to grow up,' said my mother before she could stop herself, for she didn't want her future son-in-law to know how much I could irritate her.

'I keep myself in trim,' said Syl.

'I expect you do press-ups,' said Lili, playfully pinching his upper arm. He did. I had seen him.

'You look well, Lili,' he remarked, also without warmth, and I wondered why they had ever been friends since they didn't like each other.

I drank too much at dinner and missed whole stretches of conversation, noting at one point with tipsy clarity that people who could converse were a great boon to the inarticulate who yet, when in the company of their tongue-tied fellows, felt it essential to say something. As it was, Lili chatted easily and Robert timed his eating to synchronise with her fluency; when Lili stopped talking to eat he carried on, not in the same vein but sufficiently in harmony with her style not to upset the balance of conviviality.

I found it curious that when everyone had finished

Robert still had a plateful of food before him and we had to wait as he ate it and Lili talked and smoked her endless cigarettes. None the less I had found the evening reassuring and felt no difficulty in saying that I was sorry but I was suddenly most awfully tired and if no one minded I thought I would go to bed.

Lili said that of course I must, but I made the error of looking at my mother for approval, found none and saw only displeasure at my childish crudity.

It was this that made me unable to sleep, so that coming downstairs, parched with alcohol, for a glass of lemonade, I heard my mother and Lili talking. Syl had left and Robert gone to bed and the old school friends were talking as they must have talked in their manless dormitory: my mother careful, Lili dashing.

My mother said, 'I've never discussed anything with her, I'm afraid. *You* know ...'

Lili said, 'You don't imagine she's a virgin, do you?'

My mother said, 'Lili, you can't be suggesting that Syl ...'

And Lili said, 'Darling, you can be so stupid sometimes.'

I went back upstairs, drank water in my hands from the bath tap and slept without dreaming.

*

At breakfast Lili for some reason spoke of fidelity, and I noted my mother as she went in and out with bread and boiling water, looking at her, not with the disapproval she reserved for me but with half-amused incredulity.

'You see,' said Lili, 'there's no real experience to be gained by promiscuity. We're all called to understand ourselves, and to do this it's necessary that we should understand one another, and this is only possible after a

28

long while of living together. Leaping from bed to be done learns nothing of any depth.'

'What have you learned, Lili?' asked my mother, at last sitting down with a cup of tea before her.

'You challenge me,' said Lili. 'What have I learned? What have I learned of myself from learning through Robert ...?

Her husband lowered his paper and regarded her over the top of it.

'I don't know,' she admitted. 'But I've learned something. Isn't it obvious that too many relationships will teach one nothing except that men are much alike?'

My mother sniffed. She had no very high opinion of men.

'So are women,' said Robert, turning back to the paper.

Lili looked affronted. 'I am quite unlike other women,' she observed.

'Yes, you are,' agreed her husband, and Lili smiled.

I thought that Robert loved her and wouldn't mind her having lovers if she always came back to him. I wondered how it was possible to love many men when you had once loved one more than your immortal soul, and whether Lili had ever loved like that, or whether this was a torment saved for ridiculous people like myself.

'What are you thinking about, Margaret?' asked Lili.

'I was thinking about what you were saying,' I told her, while memories of Nour flooded my being so that I felt I couldn't bear it but must instantly take that gleaming knife and open my body to let him out.

'I sometimes talk nonsense,' said Lili, 'and sometimes I don't. Mostly I don't, but you must be careful when you listen to me.'

'*Don't* fill her head with a lot of nonsense,' said my mother, rather oddly since, on the face of it, Lili had been recommending the path of virtue. I understood that my

29

mother was ambivalent about marriage, bitter about her own experience of it while seeing no possible alternative for me, and that this must make things difficult for her.

She said that sensible people weren't led astray by infatuation. She implied that only a fool could allow what was known as 'love' to enter into consideration in the matter. She stated that a wise woman would choose her mate on the basis of his qualities of character.

Lili's cigarette smoke went down the wrong way. 'Nobody ever married anyone because he was virtuous,' she protested. Then she recanted. 'Yes they did. What nobody ever did was go to bed with someone because he was virtuous.'

My mother looked annoyed and inclined to dispute this but, naturally, she couldn't. What could she say?

There was still so much I didn't understand. The revelations of evil that I had experienced had brought me only to confusion and powerlessness. I remembered a night by the river when daylight faded, darkness fell and the moon rose at once with a new light and I had thought I understood everything and that everything was good. Now I knew myself to be bad in a bad world, a vessel of poison afloat in a sea of poison, and I thought that this was all there was to know.

'We have to go into town,' said Lili. 'I'm going to take Margaret with us.'

I protested. I wanted only to go down to the summer-house and watch the leaves falling until night fell with them.

'You go,' said my mother decisively. 'It'll do you good.'

That was that, for if I now refused my mother would see to it that I regretted my foolishness.

'What are you going to wear?' asked Lili.

'Wear your grey tweed,' advised my mother. 'You look nice in that.'

'Let me look,' said Lili. 'I adore other people's wardrobes.'

She looked through my chest-of-drawers after she had decided that the grey tweed would do.

'Haven't you got a grey jumper?' she enquired. 'How elegant you would look all in grey – like a little nun.'

Elegance was not a concept I associated with myself, nor with nuns, but as I thought about it I realised that Lili was right. The sisters had indeed looked most neat and lovely in their colourless habits, stark against the brightness of the country.

'She should wear a red jumper,' objected my mother. 'A nice colourful contrast.'

'No, no,' said Lili. 'That is a very English notion and quite misplaced. I shall lend her a jumper. She shall go all in grey and you shall lend her your seed pearls. Now a pale lipstick and some powder and she can slip into Bond Street without looking as though she came from Croydon.'

'She does come from Croydon,' said my mother.

'There's no need for her to *look* as though she does,' said Lili.

My mother, in her mustard-coloured coat and skirt, with a green jumper for her nice colourful contrast, looked minutely offended but wasn't sufficiently interested in clothes to argue the matter further. 'She'll look very drab,' was all she said.

Lili brushed my hair with a brush wrapped in a silk scarf and pinched my upper lip to refine the line of lipstick.

'You must never underestimate the power of clothes,' she said. 'Clothes *are* the person. Take away the clothes and you take away the personality. Naked people are nothing. You wouldn't recognise me if you met me in the bath.'

I thought of the river and Nour.

My mother said, 'Since you're so mad about clothes, Lili, you can help me alter the wedding dress.'

'OK,' said Lili nonchalantly.

31

Someone had lent Robert a car. He had the expatriate knack of being lent things and getting himself looked after on his return to the native land, and as they talked it became apparent that we were to be entertained to lunch by the gallery owner.

'Won't he mind if I come too?' I asked.

'I don't care if he does,' said Robert rather ungallantly.

'No one cares about *him*,' said Lili.

My heart misgave me. Together with the other pains of youth, I was shy.

'We were going to stay with him,' said Lili, 'but it's much nicer staying with you. The least he can do is buy us a decent lunch.'

I wondered if Lili and Robert were short of money since his government had impoverished Lili's father. I had the impression that unless you were famous there was little money to be made from art.

I asked, 'Is it difficult to sell paintings?', thinking this a quite decorous way of framing my question.

'Yes,' said Robert.

'Not if you know how,' said Lili. 'I shall sell a lot at the opening. I shall spike the wine and tell people how beautiful they are.' She sounded excited at the prospect, alert, like any animal at the beginning of something – a race, a hunt, a battle.

'How beautiful who are?' asked Robert.

'The people and the paintings, of course,' said Lili. 'I must flatter people and arouse their acquisitive instincts at one and the same time.'

'You're good at that,' said Robert, but he didn't sound, as I thought he might have done, condemnatory.

'I enjoy it,' said Lili. 'It's good for *me*. It gives me a role in life. A positive helpmeet to my husband. Now if you were rich I should have nothing to do. I should be a silent shell,

32

wealthy and withered and bored. As it is, I have been forced into positive action, into vitality and life.'

She spoke to her husband, but I thought she was addressing me, for he must have heard this before, or at least known what was in her mind.

He said mildly, 'I always told you you shouldn't have given up dancing.'

Lili said, 'I was tired of dancing. I wanted to stay with you, not go all round the world, dancing.'

'You wouldn't have gone round the world,' said Robert. 'Summer seasons in Fayyum perhaps.'

Lili laughed.

I thought – if it had been my parents who had been talking, they would have been doing it at the tops of their voices, for surely on the content alone that conversation had been a row. I wondered whether Robert and Lili had spoken so often like this that neither had any longer the energy to shout, or whether there never had been anger between them. They were quite outside my experience. It was as though they were creatures of the same species, possessed of a venom which might kill an outsider, but were powerless to injure each other.

'If I had been married to a successful man,' said Lili, 'I should never have discovered myself, or my potential.'

'You've always been the same, Lili,' said Robert. He was right, for I remembered her and she hadn't changed.

*

The gallery owner sighed when he saw us. Only I saw him sigh, for Lili and Robert were looking not at him but at the walls, and he found me too negligible to bother to disguise his ennui.

'Robert, Lili,' he said and didn't enquire as to my identity.

33

'This is Margaret,' said Lili abstractedly. 'I don't know why you were worried about the lighting, Robert.'

'It glares off the surface,' said Robert.

'No it doesn't,' said Lili. 'Not if you stand here.'

'Everyone won't be able to stand there,' said Robert. 'Not if you're standing there.'

'I have booked a table for midday,' said the gallery owner, 'and I have an appointment at two.'

As we walked to the restaurant I felt miserable, foreseeing argument and dissent and wishing that I possessed the charm and the experienced polish to ease the tension between these people.

Lili said suddenly, 'What I like best in the world is to see *men* dancing.'

Robert said, 'I was telling Lili in the car that she shouldn't have stopped being a dancer.'

'I don't mean ballet,' said Lili. 'I gave up ballet because I found the artifice irksome. It isn't natural to dance on one's toes. People can't fly, they can only jump, and once you've realised that you must either laugh or cry. I like to see men stamping all of their foot on the ground – Morris dancers and Russians and Greeks – and jumping, like people who are resigned to mere jumping, without any pretence at flight. I don't think I like to see women dancing at all – when they're not hopping they're undulating.'

'Don't you enjoy the ballet?' asked the gallery owner, who, I think, had not been listening.

'*No*,' said Lili with emphatic patience. 'I dislike the artifice, you see.'

'You must suspend disbelief,' advised the gallery owner, bored.

'I don't see why I should,' said Lili, argumentative.

She stopped walking suddenly, so that two people behind nearly collided with her. We also stopped after a few paces and turned to look back at her. She seemed poised to make a speech, then and there, in the middle of Tottenham Court Road, but all she said, before she came forward to join us, was: 'Art can be a snare and a delusion.'

'If it wasn't for art,' said Robert, 'we wouldn't be about to eat.'

We had reached the restaurant, and the gallery owner held the door open for us as we went in. It was called El Misr and Lili exclaimed, 'Egypt again. Egypt is surely the motif of the year.'

'I thought it would make you feel at home,' said the gallery owner – untruthfully, I felt. I suspected that the restaurant was cheap and that this was the reason we had been guided here. Also I could hear irony in his tone and I thought that for some reason he was very annoyed indeed.

I could hear foreign voices raised in the kitchen and stopped listening to my companions. When I again became conscious of what they were saying I heard Lili arguing. '... Not soft and soggy,' she was saying.

I must have looked enquiring, for Robert explained, 'We are debating whether beans should retain some bite.'

'It doesn't really matter,' said Lili, losing interest. 'They'll bring it the way it is anyway. They think we're stupid about food.'

I said, 'I think they're right.'

Everyone looked faintly surprised, for I hadn't previously volunteered a remark.

'Hashed mutton,' I said by way of explanation, 'and tinned spaghetti on toast.'

'Oh yes,' agreed Lili gloomily. 'No wonder the English look so awful.'

'Margaret doesn't look awful,' said Robert, as though it was expected of him.

'We,' said Lili, 'have *just* managed to force down

35

sufficient amounts of fresh veg and protein to retain some shapeliness and complexion.'

I found it odd that Robert had chosen to distinguish me alone as English and wondered how he saw himself and Lili and I found it odd that Lili had chosen to lay claim to Englishness. I hadn't yet learned that she was able to change her nationality as she changed her accessories, to suit the occasion. She was skilled at being English, but she was more interesting when she was half Arab.

They talked about art, and I drank too much because I had nothing to say. I felt that my life fitted me as ill as a garment designed for somebody else.

*

I don't know how I got the following impression from Lili. I don't believe I was listening to her very closely. Not listening was always one of my faults and one of the reasons I so frequently found myself isolated in misunderstanding: like a careless rider, cut off from the company, alone and benighted for failing to pay attention to the prevailing agreements as to intention and direction. After a while the other riders don't even bother to come and look for you. They leave you to amble into the desert on your own, and when you come to think of it you can't really blame them.

One day she was talking about love again. She said – or I heard – that we should only fall in love once, that it was an experience of such profound significance that to repeat it would be to devalue it. This seemed to me so true that I couldn't imagine why it was not universally acknowledged. Even in my limited experience I had seen people falling in and out of love, as though, soiled by sorrow and loss, they had to go in search of comfort from one used and lukewarm bath to another. The marriage service, I conceded, did

36

insist on exclusivity, but clearly people other than myself were prone to not listening. It was sad for me that I had fallen in love with someone who did not love me, but it was not an experience I cared to repeat – for more and better reasons than the fear of pain. If it had been an illusion, then other illusions lay ahead, a hall of mirrors, a series of mirages. I had lost faith, not in God but in the carnal love which so preoccupied almost everyone I had ever known. How they talked and sang and wrote and thought about it, as though union with another were the entire purpose of existence. And how could they believe it when disillusion, of one sort or another, sooner or later was the almost invariable result? Perhaps it was not I but the other riders who were hell-bent on the wrong route. I was too unsure of myself to believe that this could be possible. Mother Joseph seemed utterly remote, her voice lost in the clamour of my mother's voice, my mother's certainty that only marriage represented sanity, security, good behaviour in a dangerous world of hostile winds and people who were 'not one of us', talking to themselves. It couldn't be that I was right, and while I yearned to return to a certainty I already knew, I heard only my mother's voice, insisting, on one dead note, that she knew of what life should consist. All the other voices around me were saying the same and the distant peal of the convent bell mingling, not incongruously, with the cry from the minaret went unheeded.

When Lili stopped speaking I wished I could ask her to repeat what she had said, but already she was lighting a cigarette and talking about linen.

'I've never seen the point of keeping piles of the stuff,' she said. 'It goes yellow if you keep it for too long and I don't see how anyone can be expected to use fifty tablecloths even in a lifetime – not mucky-looking yellow ones. And where are you supposed to keep them all?'

37

'I don't know,' I said. I already had a great many tablecloths in boxes with bows on. Presents from relations.

'There'd be no room for one's clothes,' said Lili, 'not with all those tablecloths and napkins.'

'The nuns have three habits,' I said. 'One to wear, one in the wash and one in the wardrobe.'

'I wouldn't mind that,' said Lili. 'It is possible to look very beautiful in a habit.'

'The habits are blessed when they make their final vows,' I said. 'They have a robing ceremony.'

'I know,' said Lili.

I knew it was probable that she knew. I just wanted to talk about it. 'Inside the main door there's a holy water stoup of blue-and-white porcelain,' I said. 'They brought it from France. The walls of the visitors' parlour are blue, and the rest are white.'

'And a statue of Our Lady in a blue-and-white dress with a golden crown,' said Lili.

I realised that I had been talking about the convent without explanation or location. 'Did you know Mother Joseph?' I asked, 'and Sister Bridget?'

'A long time ago,' said Lili, 'when we used to stay with Marie Claire.'

My mother had come in. 'Wasted lives,' she said. She was a very English Catholic and opposed to religious excess in all its forms.

I wanted to ask whether she thought her own life unwasted and whether the fact that she had given birth to me was sufficient justification for it.

'I don't think so,' said Lili. 'I should have liked to be a nun, except they wouldn't have let me smoke and I couldn't live without cigarettes. I wouldn't want to.'

'*You*?' said my mother. 'A fine nun you'd have made.' She moved to empty the ashtray. I thought, Be still and I am God. 'Some of them are very good and quite useful, but it's a selfish existence.'

*

'I don't want to appear awkward,' said Lili that evening, 'but she looks like something the cat dragged in.' She was sitting on her heels with a pin in her mouth, eyeing me with pity as I stood yet again in my mother's wedding dress.

'That's why I want to alter it,' explained my mother wearily, too tired to argue.

'I'm not certain that it's salvageable,' said Lili.

'That's rubbish,' said my mother. 'It's in perfect condition. All it needs is to be made to fit. It looked lovely on me.'

'Hmm,' said Lili abstractedly, leaning forward and tweaking at the hem. The fact that she was doing this and not looking at her old friend made her doubts about this statement less evident, but all the same my mother protested. 'It *did*, Lili,' she said. 'Everyone said so.'

'Oh yes, it did,' said Lili, 'though, mind you, I think it highly unlikely that anyone would tell you on your wedding day that you looked the most frightful frump – not,' she added hastily, 'that you did. All I mean is that brides are always described as beautiful.'

She sat back on her heels again. 'They so seldom are,' she reflected. 'Tulle is terrible, and lace is worse, and white is woeful. Nothing white should ever be taken in at the waist. White should either flow in an unbroken line from the shoulder to the ground or be superbly cut and tailored. Veils don't help. They make the poor girls look as though they hadn't been properly unpacked, as though they'd been taken out of the box and someone had left half their wrappings on.'

39

'I don't know why you have to be so contrary,' snapped my mother. 'Brides always wear white and veils. They always have.'

'Murder is fairly common too,' said Lili. 'It always has been.'

'Don't be silly, Lili,' said my mother. 'The white is meant to represent purity and innocence.'

'That's pretty stupid,' said Lili, 'considering that marriage means an end to all that. I can see why nuns wear white when they take the veil, but when you think of the way everyone goes on at the prospect of the wedding night innocence is the last thing on anyone's mind.' She now had a cigarette between her teeth and squinted against the smoke.

'Don't be disgusting,' said my mother.

'There you are,' said Lili. '*You* said disgusting.'

'Oh, anyway,' said my mother, 'I don't know why we're talking about it. She's got to wear that dress, come what may.'

'Why?' asked Lili.

'Because I wore it,' explained my mother. 'I've saved it for years for my daughter to wear.'

I thought she might add, 'And she's bloody well going to wear it', but my mother had said her piece for the moment. Her insistence seemed absurd in view of her own failed marriage, but I had always been too nervous to point this out, to ask what she made of the break in connection between the symbolism of the dress and the unassailability of the marriage vow.

'I wore crimson at my wedding,' said Lili. 'Heavy wild silk, calf-length.'

'I know,' said my mother acidly. 'I was there.'

'I looked *wonderful*,' remarked Lili dreamily. 'I should have been marrying a prince.'

My mother said nothing, and Lili stubbed out her cigarette in a pin tray. She said, 'Well, if there's nothing else for it', and began to fold and manipulate the wedding dress while I stood like a doll, cold and alien and powerless.

*

That night my mother went to bed early and Robert walked through the wood, past the golf course to the pub. He would pass Syl's house on the way, since it stood close to ours on the same side of the private road, behind hedges of cypress and box, flanked by lawns garnished with birch and all manner of ornamental trees.

'Why don't you pop in and see Syl and say hello to his mother?' suggested Lili, malice flickering in her bright face.

'He'll be busy,' said Robert, 'studying briefs, or whatever it is he does.'

'Oh, go on,' said Lili. 'He'll be delighted to have a break and go off for a pint. Perhaps he'll play you a tune on his oboe.' Syl's oboe was another of the things about him that I couldn't bear. He must have been playing the beastly thing for years.

'I'll see,' said Robert – I think in deference to me, for he gave his wife a nasty look as she beamed up at him.

I thought – it isn't just me. Nobody likes Syl. I'm marrying a man whom nobody likes. I could see the room beginning to spin as though I had had a dreadful shock or a moment of unbearable fear. That I myself did not like Syl was almost immaterial, since I deserved nothing better, but even with my penitential self-disgust it seemed unfair to me, and otiose, that my future husband should be so generally unpopular. With a glimmer of self-preservation I began to reason that to be a martyr to an unwanted marriage was one thing, whereas to look like a fool in the eyes of all the

41

world was another. Then I suddenly saw that Syl, too, must look a very great fool, for he was twice my age and I wasn't beautiful, nor talented, nor in the least degree interesting. We were, I suddenly perceived, an entirely incongruous and idiotic couple. I thought that he was already a man when I was born, that he had seen me growing up, and I thought of the strange, sad, frightening creatures who haunted the borders of the woods watching the children play.

'Oh Lili,' I said, and I grasped the table's edge.

Her expression, to my fearful eyes, was enigmatic. It might have been compassionate, or amused, or even hostile.

She lit a cigarette, and when she spoke her tone was cool. 'Sometimes there are things you have to do,' she said, 'and sometimes there aren't. Sometimes other people can make up your mind for you and sometimes they can't. Sometimes you have to grow up – not just once but all through your life. Even very old people sometimes have to suddenly grow up a bit.'

I didn't really understand what she was saying, but I could see that she despised me.

'You think I'm stupid,' I said.

'No I don't,' said Lili. 'I think you've lost hope, and the only thing I can tell you is that if you hang on hope will come back, and you mustn't do anything until it does.'

My wedding was close. Would hope return in time?

'I've got to go through with it now,' I said.

'Oh well,' said Lili.

She seemed again to have lost interest, in that swift way she had, and I felt useless and bereft.

'Tired,' said Lili. 'Bed.'

*

42

The next day was Saturday, and Syl called in the middle of the morning. He had been playing golf and was wearing cavalry-twill trousers and a plaid tie round an unbuttoned shirt-neck.

'How boyish and negligent you look,' cried Lili.

She reminded me of a wasp as she flitted round him, a wasp suddenly aware, in the way wasps have, that there is rotting matter in the vicinity, for she had been upstairs when he arrived by way of the garden and couldn't have seen him.

'I've been noticing how very much roof you have,' she said to my mother. 'I've never known a house with so much roof. In places it almost comes down to the ground.'

'It was designed like that,' said my mother, 'on purpose.'

'But why?' asked Lili.

'I don't know why,' said my mother. 'It must have been some idea the architect had. Does it matter?'

'No, it doesn't *matter*,' said Lili. 'It just seems so peculiar.'

'It's no more peculiar than the other houses on the drive,' argued my mother, and she was right. Ours was glancingly Tudorbethan and called 'The Oaks'; others had clearly been inspired by visits to Spain and were called '*Casa*-something-or-other'; one or two bore hints of castellation and crenellation and were appropriately named after some of the statelier English homes; while Syl's house had been conceived in a dour Regency style by a less fertile imagination and its grey dressed stones were covered by a great pelt of ivy. It was the only house on the drive that I could imagine Syl's mother living in. The haciendas, the castles and the oast-houses would not have suited her at all.

'I wonder what it's worth now?' mused Lili, scandalizing my mother. 'It's much too big for you. Why don't you sell it?'

'It's my home,' said my mother stiffly.

'Oh silly,' said Lili. 'You sound as though your family had lived here since Sir Eggleswyke slew the great eel.'

'I came here as a bride,' said my mother, and Lili giggled.

My mother had insisted when my father left that she should keep the house, and all its contents, and continue to receive a major part of his income. I felt guilty about sharing in this bounty, for my stepmother and her children could clearly have benefited from some of it.

'And I couldn't now adapt,' said my mother, sounding grand, 'to a smaller house.'

Nor could she then justify employing a cleaner and the odd-job man who kept all the local gardens more or less under control. Nothing would persuade my mother to lower her standards, for that might ease my father's lot.

'Well, the place certainly suits you,' said Lili – I thought ambiguously, but my mother looked gratified.

'It would be foolish to sell now,' said Syl judiciously, and I thought that apart from wanting young girls he wanted to inherit another big house, and I wondered how on earth I could be going to marry someone whom I detested so much.

'Why did you disappear like that?' he asked.

I had left the room without speaking and gone into the garden. Now he stood behind me, so that I could feel the warmth of his body, but I was facing the box hedge, so close to it that I couldn't turn.

'I won't marry you,' I said. My voice was high and it shook and I didn't convince even myself.

'Yes, you will,' said Syl.

He sounded like my mother at that moment and I was surprised, for I had thought him weak. I saw that I was intended to be subject to people like these two, was doomed to marry Syl as surely as I had been born of my mother.

'You and your little nerves,' he said and he put his fingers

44

in the back of the collar of my dress and pulled it slightly as
though I was a recalcitrant dog.

I didn't like to be touched by almost anyone. I said, 'Let
me go, Syl', because I felt ridiculous, crushed between this
man and the garden hedge. I spoke calmly since now
revulsion had given way to hopelessness. I had remembered
the last time I had stood in a garden with a man.

'I don't love you, Syl,' I said. He stood back and let me
turn. I looked at his face, which was something I did
seldom, for I didn't like it, and saw that he didn't believe
me; that he found it inconceivable that I shouldn't love
him; that, ageing and unmarried though he was, he
believed himself to be irresistible.

I stepped round him and went back to the house.

Lili was alone in the sitting-room. I wanted to tell her
that I had told Syl I wouldn't marry him, but I didn't, for I
felt that once I had told Lili she would somehow prevent me
from recanting and that, freed from Syl, I should be bound
even tighter to my mother.

There was a hangnail at the side of my thumb and now I
took it between my teeth and tore it off so that the blood
ran, leaving a scarlet spotting on my dress where it bloused
out above my waist.

'That's attractive,' remarked Lili, regarding it distaste-
fully. 'Spilt blood is quite the untidiest thing I can think of –
much worse than milk.'

I sucked my thumb and mumbled that I hadn't meant to
do it.

'You've probably ruined that dress,' said Lili, and I said
it didn't matter.

'Come to the kitchen quickly,' she said, getting to her
feet.

She took one of my mother's gingham breakfast napkins
from a drawer and wrung it out in cold water.

'You keep your thumb in your mouth,' she advised, 'and I'll try and get these stains out.'

'What have you done?' asked my mother from the doorway, her arms full of branches of copper-beech.

'It's all right,' said Lili. 'Not a road accident. She just bit her nail.'

'Well, don't soak her,' said my mother. 'She'll get pneumonia. How did she bite her nail?'

Lili regarded her, her head tilted thoughtfully.

'Like this,' she said after a moment, gripping her own thumbnail between her back teeth and worrying at it.

'It was a hangnail,' I explained. 'I pulled it off and it bled.'

'You'll get blood poisoning if you're not careful,' said my mother, putting her leaves on the draining-board.

I wondered, since my mother was principally concerned for my health, and Lili only for my dress, why it was that I had felt secure until my mother arrived.

'There,' said Lili after a final rub. 'There may be a mark, but it won't show too badly. You'd better find a plaster for that thumb or it might start bleeding again.'

It was a very small wound to have caused such concern. That night by the river there had been so much blood …

'It's nothing to cry about,' said my mother contemptuously, and I said that I wasn't crying. Lili agreed with me, saying that a reddened nose didn't count as crying, not in her book.

'I have a good cry sometimes,' she said, 'in the same way that I sometimes have a spring-clean. I close the house and take the phone off the hook and I cry.'

'Why?' asked my mother.

'It's good for me,' explained Lili. 'You should try it yourself. It would do you the world of good.'

'I can't think what you've got to cry about,' said my

mother, managing to imply that she herself had far more to cry about than Lili and far too much strength of character to do so.

'All living beings,' said Lili, 'have something to cry about.'

I could tell by her voice that she had just said something which she believed, and I was surprised, because I had somehow thought her too clever really to believe anything.

'Sometimes,' she said, 'I sink into a grand black horror of depression, but I don't cry so much then. I stay in bed and pluck at the counterpane and listen to the winds of solitude roaring at the edge of infinity and the wolves of evil baying down the void, and I look into the darkness.'

My mother obviously considered this to be both morbid and affected. 'For goodness sake, Lili,' she said, 'do try and say something cheerful.'

'I can't think of anything just at present,' said Lili. 'Can you?'

'The wedding of course,' said my mother ill-advisedly.

Lili frowned, and I wondered what would happen if I should say that the wedding was cancelled.

'It's going to be so jolly,' said my mother.

Lili and I were silent and I wondered for a moment how I would be feeling if I was going to marry the man I loved – *had* loved, I amended in my mind, for surely even I couldn't be so idiotic as to love still where I had met with such treachery. But I could. I was sufficiently idiotic to love with a longing that weakened me as though I was bleeding.

'We're having *canapés*,' said my mother doggedly, 'and asparagus rolls and *vols-au-vent*.'

'Of course,' said Lili, 'and champagne and speeches and confetti.' Her tone was flat and glum and my mother looked at her suspiciously.

'What's wrong with that?' she asked.

'Nothing, nothing,' said Lili, 'only I do hate weddings. I wish I'd had a gypsy wedding, jumping over the fire and fleeing into the night.'

'You'd have burned your red frock,' said my mother acidly.

'Then Robert would have stamped out the flames and carried me still smouldering into the thicket.'

'Robert would have turned the fire extinguisher on you,' said my mother with what I thought was unusual perception.

'Well, then I should have married some gypsy who would have trodden all over the fire with his bare feet,' said Lili. 'One with earrings and a spotted scarf.'

'I thought Robert was the only man in the world for you,' observed my mother.

'He is,' said Lili. 'I was toying with fantasy.'

'You do too much of that,' said my mother, putting the kettle on. If she had seen the man I loved she would have thought him a figure of fantasy too. Foreign, unsuitable. And, I admitted to myself, she would have been absolutely right.

'When is Derek coming?' asked Lili, perhaps because we were on the subject of husbands.

'The night before the wedding,' said my mother without much enthusiasm. 'We're having drinks here in the evening.'

'No stag-night for Syl?' asked Lili.

'Of course not,' said my mother.

'I suppose he's a bit old for that sort of thing,' said Lili, 'although with that ridiculous car he drives he does seem to be trying to give an impression of boyish insouciance.'

My mother ignored this, while I felt myself flush with vicarious embarrassment. Syl went out of his way to preserve a semblance of youthfulness, wearing his clothes

48

untidily and even eating in a haphazard fashion as though he wasn't quite old enough to have learned proper manners. He liked to be the centre of attention and would sulk in any gathering where people talked and laughed without him.

'And you must go to confession,' my mother told me.

I knew that.

*

Our Irish priest was not a person I felt I could unburden myself to. He was quite aware of my childish misdemeanours, but I hadn't been to confession since I returned from Egypt, and I thought he would be profoundly shocked by what I should have to tell him. He came several times a year to have a glass of sherry with my mother and I always felt awkward in his presence, fearing that instead of 'Would you care for an olive?' I might remark 'Bless me, Father, for I have sinned'. At the sight of him I would smell the dust of the confessional and remember the mixture of boredom, shame and relief as I said my penances. I was familiar with the view that the priesthood is beyond shock, being entirely cognisant of the whole sum of human folly and evil from the outpourings of the penitent, but I wasn't convinced. I also had a feeling that my mother would never forgive me if she thought I had admitted to fornication and worse to a person who came to her house and drank her sherry. I sometimes thought that the social considerations of people like my mother militated more against religion than atheism or simple sin. I had discovered in Egypt what seemed like a different religion: a thing of unimaginable heights and depths, of light and shadow with none of the vertiginous darkness of which Lili had spoken. Now that I was home, my religion seemed

49

compounded of polite appearances and the prospect of eternal Hell. It was unfortunate, I thought, that at the same time as I had realised the grandeur of God I had fallen in love with a mortal, and that the two experiences should have proved to be mutually exclusive, leaving me with the sensation that I was being sundered by equal forces. Destroyed.

I went to confession. I took the bus to the neighbouring parish and told an unseen, unknown priest all that had happened. A sad little tale it sounded, a trivial matter to consign a soul to perpetual separation. I felt apologetic for boring the poor man and was as brief as possible in order to spare, not myself, but him. Afterwards I had no sense that I had been forgiven, but I had done what I was called upon to do and there it must rest.

I told my mother where I had been without explanation as to why I had chosen not to go to our own church, and she said nothing. I wondered whether she believed in God. I knew that she didn't believe in him as I did because in that case I would have recognised her as I had recognised Mother Joseph, who inhabited a territory which I had visited. My mother, I felt sure, had never been there. She had no travellers' tales, no air of a person who had been on a journey, and I knew she would be both disbelieving and resentful if I should try to describe the eternal vistas I had glimpsed. To her, religion was morality and appearance, and she kept it in the same compartment of her mind as her dinner napkins. Suspicious of excess and what she thought of as theatricality, she lived – quite adequately and blamelessly – on the lowest level of religious experience. If I should cry, trying to express the inexpressible, that I had walked the wind with archangels, she would have been worried and annoyed; and if I had gone on to say that I had forfeited those heights and lived now in an unremitting shadowless glare of exposure in a runnel of Hell, she would have feared for my mental health. I did myself.

'I like to go to confession straight after I've been to the hairdresser,' said Lili. 'It makes me feel so complete, body and soul.'

'I don't think you've got quite the right idea, Lili,' said my mother.

'Yes, I have. It's all about ease, you see,' said Lili.

My mother looked irritable. She subscribed on the face of it to the proposition that we are not put here to be happy, although she was the first to complain if she, or the few people she loved, were not. Lili, the hedonist, on the other hand, was clearly familiar with some of the regions of Hell. She had described them earlier and I had known what she meant.

*

That night I was again subjected to the ordeal by wedding dress. I imagined what would happen if I should tear the sleeves out, or cut it up, or run to the kitchen for the tomato-ketchup and pour it all over the bodice; if I should rip out the collar with my teeth. I could hear the sound of rent cloth in my head, but I stood on a wooden chair while Lili pinned the seams closer, standing quietly like a broken horse to be saddled and bridled. Bridalled and saddled. I said: 'I feel sick.'

'Don't be silly,' said my mother.

I wished I did feel sick. I wished I could be sick on my mother's wedding dress.

'It's beginning to fit much better,' said my mother.

When I tried to take it off I found that Lili had pinned it to my petticoat and I was trapped in it.

'Well, *what* a performance,' remarked my mother rather

breathlessly after a short urgent scene.

Lili watched me thoughtfully as I put on my skirt and blouse. I was shaking and my eyes were blurred.

The dress lay on the floor and my mother picked it up tenderly, as though it was a child. I think she may even have said a few words to it.

'Robert will be getting lonely,' said Lili. 'Downstairs all on his own.'

'You can join him now,' said my mother. 'I think it fits as well as it ever will. We'll all go down and have a martini.'

I could smell a sour smell of old cloth, of old weddings, old sorrows.

'I could do with a whisky,' I said.

'I hope you're not becoming an alcoholic,' said my mother with the unfairness of the recently offended.

'She's got some way to go,' said Lili. 'Unlike me. I often fear I drink too much.'

'Nonsense,' said my mother tartly, as though she thought Lili was showing off.

'You are not of that opinion?' enquired Lili, her head tilted in a way that I was beginning to be familiar with. 'You have no fears for *ma foi*?'

'I've got better things to worry about,' said my mother, not letting us forget for a moment her onerous wedding duties. 'Margaret has to have tea with Syl's mother tomorrow.'

She spoke as one implying, 'And serve her damn well right.'

'I do think she might have offered to do something to help, but then it's always up to the bride's mother to make the arrangements, even when she's on her own.'

The implication here was that Syl's mother was very much richer than mine and a mean old beast.

'It's the convention, my poor duck,' said Lili. 'You like convention.'

52

My mother looked as though she wasn't too keen on this one. 'Syl is very good,' she said, consoling herself. 'Where's your ring?'

I said I thought it too valuable to wear constantly and had put it in my dressing-table drawer. My poor mother, I am sure, couldn't determine whether to commend my prudence or berate me for my lack of romance. I hated the hoop of diamonds which, although I had washed it, looked somehow dirty. It reposed in a box of plum velvet on a bed of harsh white satin, reminding me, whenever I saw it, of the inherent vulgarity of marriage, that combination of contract and concupiscence.

'What are you doing about your going-away clothes?' demanded my mother.

I had promised to go round the shops looking for something suitable, since my mother had shown that she wished to accompany me. I had said that I would find it easier on my own and she had been hurt, for normal mothers and daughters went together on this expedition, lunching in a department store and discussing the newly acquired contents of the carrier bags that lay at their feet. My trousseau had been taken care of already – underwear, nightgowns and some light dresses for my honeymoon. I had said that we should go to Egypt for this, not believing that the occasion would ever really arise; that I should be married to Syl and taken to the country in which I had come to life and lost it. My perversity had seemed to me amusing. I didn't even realise how unhappy I was, as the wounded suffer merciful shock.

'You are such a lump,' said my mother ill-temperedly. 'You don't enjoy anything.'

'Pity she couldn't get her clothes in Cairo,' said Lili.

'She didn't think of that,' said my mother.

'She didn't know then she was going to get married,' said

Lili – on the face of it reasonably.

But I had thought I was, though not to Syl. Not to Syl. By now I was past weeping.

'Why aren't you seeing Syl this evening?' asked my mother, who knew.

'He has to see a man,' I reminded her tonelessly.

Now my mother did something rather risky. She said, at the end of her patience, 'Don't you love Syl?'

And I said smoothly that of course I did, for I wasn't going to be inveigled into an emotional uproar.

'Love?' said Lili sardonically. 'What's love?'

'I thought you knew,' said my mother. 'I thought you were the expert.'

Lili must also have realised that here was thin ice: thin ice over deep waters.

'I know absolutely nothing about it,' she said airily, dismissing the subject.

My mother looked dissatisfied, but I switched off my bedroom light and we were moving downstairs towards Robert and the tray of martinis.

*

Tea with Syl's mother was a taxing experience. She had a little pug-like dog who wore an expression of perpetual outrage, its eyes bulging as though someone had just said something unforgivable to it. She and this animal treated each other with mutual contempt, like an old unhappily married couple, and I always thought that the only reason he didn't bite her or she have him put down was that they disliked the rest of the world even more than each other and would have been even more miserable and lonely than they were in their trap of hostility.

'Cootchy, cootchy, coo,' said Lili to the dog. She had insisted on coming with me to refresh, so she said, her memory of that ghastly old trout. Syl's mother was highly displeased to see her and made a great to-do of fetching an extra cup, saucer and plate, worrying aloud that there wouldn't be enough for three of us to eat.

Anchovy-paste sandwiches, scones and Dundee cake seemed to me an ample repast, particularly as I had a nervous, irrational distaste for eating the food of Syl's mother in her house. I crumbled a scone and left the raisins and crumbs all over my plate.

Syl's mother disapproved of this most bitterly and rebuked me for waste.

'You should empty the teapot over the old horror's head,' suggested Lili when our hostess had gone to replenish the jug of milk.

I said, 'Ssshh', cravenly, for I was scared of her, although not as scared as I was of my own parent.

Lili had already smoked three cigarettes and stubbed them out in her saucer, devil-may-care, and Mrs Monro had said nothing. Now she jabbed the toe of her smart Italian shoe in the dog, who was snuffling about under the table. We were sitting in the window embrasure looking out over the laurustines, cupressus and other seemingly indestructible plants.

'Bugger off,' said Lili to the dog, incurring the insincere wrath of his mistress, who chose that moment to reappear.

'He was making love to my foot,' explained Lili.

'He's not capable of that,' said Syl's mother with a Yorkhire accent.

She seldom sounded Yorkshire and I had never known her to make a joke. For an instant I saw a different woman: not the sour, bored old creature I had grown to expect, but someone strong and humorous. She was gone again in a flash, leaving me faintly confused and in doubt about my capacity to judge people. No one liked her, so why should I suddenly? Was it possible that people were even more complicated than I had imagined, and had Mrs Monro once been young and funny? I couldn't remember her ever having been any different, and even Lili couldn't have known her as a young woman, for Syl's mother was old enough to have been his grandmother.

'Well, he was thinking about it,' said Lili.

I would never have dared speak so, but she was quite unselfconscious, although I suspected her of an intention to shock – to shock me as much as anyone.

'You can read the minds of animals then?' said Mrs Monro, more like herself.

'Some of them – yes,' said Lili judiciously. 'Some of them are remarkably transparent. I've known horses I could read like a book. Cats aren't so easy – more opaque, you could say. Camels are unexpected, but dogs on the whole make their intentions quite plain.'

'And their likes and dislikes,' said Mrs Monro.

I envied Lili and her social skills. I felt she would be at home in an arena with starving lions. It was hard to imagine anything eating Lili, even being rude to her. Rudeness and aggression, I felt, would merely amuse her.

'I don't think he likes me,' she said of the dog. 'He is simply overwhelmed by purposeless lust.'

I hadn't noticed anything untoward in the animal's behaviour, but I believed what Lili said. She was too secure to lie, it seemed to me. Only the doubtful, those who were bad at living, needed to dissemble.

'He's old,' said Mrs Munro, and I wondered whether she was thinking of herself: that old age bred inanition, that the longer one lived the less one cared for one's fellows. With perverted hope I wondered if with time love might fail, and all the pain ease. I almost envied Mrs Monro, who couldn't now be far from blameless death, beyond desire, perhaps

56

beyond regret. I had lost all joy in youth. Mrs Monro was old, but she wasn't debilitated as I was. She had energy and opinions, and I had none. I was tired, and she was not. I was such a weary girl that I bored myself.

*

'Do you ever bore yourself?' I enquired of Lili on the way home.

'I just did,' said Lili.

'You weren't boring,' I protested, surprised.

'Yes, I was,' she said. 'I was doing a solo. I kept hearing myself uttering a light laugh.'

'I'm sorry,' I said humbly. 'I just find her so difficult to talk to. I can never think of anything to say.'

'There isn't really anything to say,' said Lili, 'not to the old. One can only talk with conviction to one's peers. Shared experience, shared uncertainties – that's the stuff of talk. General conversation is a nightmare. Gossip, that's what makes the world go round.'

My mother claimed to disapprove of gossip. I wondered what I would have been like if Lili had been my mother, but it was impossible to imagine Lili in the depths of maternity. Mothers, no matter how disparate, had something in common, some elusive quality which Lili conspicuously lacked. I pondered what this quality might be – not unselfishness, which it might have been, for I knew selfish mothers; not *gravitas*, not responsibility. I wondered if it might be an admission of mortality, an agreement that as birth precedes so death must follow. I couldn't imagine Lili dying. She was ageless and even in age would, I knew, be careless.

'I wish I was like you,' I said suddenly, still childish enough to speak like this, to say what I meant without recourse to subtlety.

'You are a bit,' said Lili.

I wasn't altogether surprised. There was about her something inhuman, and while I saw her as fey rather than remote, I was aware of my own inhumanity: something in me which was arid and incapable of desire. I wished for nothing but the absence of pain, and Lili seemed beyond harm: as secure and unassailable as the morning-star.

'But you're happy,' I said foolishly.

'I make it my business to be happy,' said Lili. 'Life is bloody awful enough without being unhappy.'

I wanted to ask her how she did it, how she attained the condition of happiness, but this question cannot be asked outright for there is no one answer. There must be a myriad ruses and devices in the pursuit of happiness, and I could think of none in order to conjure up a complementary question. I knew she liked smoking, but I did not. She took pleasure in clothes, and I did not. She liked the company of men, and I did not. Yet I knew that none of these, nor all of them, made her life complete. It seemed I could learn nothing of happiness from Lili unless I could first discover her secret. Then I could frame my question, but then, of course, I wouldn't need to. I thought that after all we weren't alike; that I was a fish, perhaps, and she a bird, and all our requirements were different. Sometimes when my mother told me how fortunate I was, how lucky to live in a nice house and be engaged to a good man, I felt like a fish in a gilded cage. It was no use her demonstrating the comfortable appointments of my environment. I was out of my element, and the air itself could have been made of gold for all the use it was to me. If I was a fish then I needed water and I had given up my right to it.

I wondered as I thought of secrets if I might find some release in telling Lili the thing that festered in my soul, and

I asked her if she would listen.

She said something I found so odd that my vision of the world faintly changed and my despair lessened. If the world was not as I perceived it then it was possible that I was not damned. I felt no great assurance of comfort, but my conviction of evil grew a little less.

She said, 'If you have a secret you don't want the world to know you must never tell it except to an enemy. And if you must tell your dearest friend your secret then you must tell others too, for inevitably the world will get to know and you will blame your dearest friend and lose him. So tell him, if you must, but also tell his brother and the butcher and the baker and the candle-stick-maker and then you will never know who has betrayed you and you can, to some degree at least, go on loving your friend. If you tell your enemy, your hatred will be even more satisfactorily justified, but the best thing to do is tell the priest. No one else. He won't tell. The trouble is, sometimes people *want* to be betrayed. It makes them feel more at home and less lonely.'

For once I listened carefully, and I understood. I would never again speak of sin, certainly not to Lili, for one of the messages I had gathered from her speech was that it would bore her. I was happy that Lili would be bored by my sin. It made it less significant. I had learned something else that I am sure she wasn't conscious of teaching me. I had learned that it was possible, if tedious, to speak of evil, but that it wasn't possible to speak clearly of God. I had no intention just then of attempting such a thing, but as I lay awake that night I realised that if it hadn't been for Lili I might have felt it necessary to attempt to describe to someone, anyone, what I knew of God and what he had asked of me. I might have felt it as a duty. Now I knew that it wasn't to be said. For one thing it was impossible to say, and for another it

59

would be a deplorable waste of time. Finally, the matter lay solely between God and me and had nothing in time or eternity to do with anyone else. So I haven't spoken of it, here or anywhere.

*

'A good time?' asked my mother when we returned.

'Oh, wonderful,' said Lili. 'What do you think?'

'I expect she gave you a good tea,' said my mother.

'I hate tea,' said Lili pettishly. 'What I want now is a good scotch and soda to take the taste away. I think she puts mothballs in her cake.'

'She buys her cake,' said my mother. 'Do you really imagine she makes it?'

'Then she shoots them in afterwards,' said Lili, 'with a special little pistol she keeps for the purpose.'

Her mood had changed again. She told my mother she had been bored silly by Mrs Monro and was tired out with making conversation. She even looked pale.

My mother was once more in a difficult position. She cared no more for Mrs Monro than did anyone else, but the mother of my groom should, by rights, be beyond criticism, a positive bonus to my marriage, and even my mother, inclined as she was, to the bright side couldn't overtly claim this. 'She's marvellous for her age,' she said.

'Oh, marvellous,' agreed Lili sarcastically. 'Can you imagine how she ever conceived Syl?'

I couldn't. I wondered what would happen if I should say that I wished she hadn't.

'Don't be coarse,' said my mother, adding, 'She's actually a very good cook. We had dinner there only a couple of weeks ago. Stew.'

'Stew,' said Lili, gloomily.

'It was all right,' protested my mother, regretting her remark about the cake.

'Was it all right, Margaret?' asked Lili, and I said I couldn't remember.

'Not that it matters,' said my mother. 'Margaret will have her own kitchen, so she'll have to learn to cook herself.'

'On a plate with parsley round,' said Lili.

'What?' asked my mother, staring.

'Cook *herself*,' said Lili. 'Oh, never mind. I shouldn't make jokes. It isn't funny.'

'Of course it isn't funny,' said my mother. 'Marriage is a serious matter.' She had again unwittingly revealed her misgivings, for on the face of it we hadn't been speaking of marriage. Hastily and irrelevantly she asserted that Mrs Monro was very fond of me.

Lili looked at her squarely, and for a moment I entertained a mad hope that she would deny this, would announce that my engagement was a travesty and a cruelty, would say that she was going to take me away and teach me how to dress or to dance. She might have done. I felt Lili might have done anything, but she didn't. She got up and poured herself a glass of whisky without asking, and my mother didn't seem to mind. She must have briefly feared what I had hoped for.

*

Robert arrived then and my mother let him in and offered him a drink.

'Hullo,' said Lili as though he were only an acquaintance. 'How did it go?'

Robert had been back to the gallery, to the annoyance, I felt sure, of the owner.

61

'It's coming together,' he said. 'Slowly.'

'Perhaps we should ask him to dinner,' said Lili.

'Who?' asked my mother, and I replied for Lili, 'Robert's gallery owner.'

As it was I who had spoken, my mother responded sharply. 'We have no time to entertain strangers at the moment.'

'I wouldn't give him a ham sandwich,' said Robert. 'He's a mean sod.'

Relieved, my mother showed some compunction. 'If it would help, we could have a simple dinner – Syl, and maybe a couple of the neighbours.'

'No point,' said Robert. 'He can hardly back out of the exhibition now.'

'Did you think he might?' asked Lili with a momentary show of anxiety.

I was surprised at this and wondered again if they were short of money.

'He always might,' said Robert, draining his glass. 'He's unpredictable, as well as mean.'

'I wouldn't let him,' said Lili. 'Just let him try.'

'Even you,' said Robert, 'could do very little to deflect him if that was his intention.'

'Watch me,' said Lili with that determined faith in herself that I found so enviable.

When she stopped talking about art, she began to talk about love. No one else had ever spoken of love in my mother's drawing-room and I imagined that Lili's conversation would cling to the curtains and the cushion covers like tobacco smoke so that the room would never be the same again.

*

Robert went away. I don't know where. I supposed that he must have heard it all before, although I didn't think he was ever bored by Lili. I knew that men didn't enjoy talk about emotion. My father had been embarrassed when my mother or I had wept at the time of his leaving. My mother had wept very little, her tears dried by her wrath, but I had cried for her.

'What are you thinking about?' asked Lili. 'I was just explaining something very important and you've got a glazed look.'

I said I was sorry.

'Lovers,' said Lili, 'lovers are even more valuable after they've stopped being lovers. One's own lover, that is. Their function is this. When you fall in love with someone new and it goes wrong you go and fetch an old lover and remember how much you loved him once and how you don't any more and can't imagine what you saw in him, and then you feel better. It's like tying an old sock round your neck when you've got a sore throat.'

'Why?' asked my mother.

'I don't know quite,' said Lili, 'but that's what it feels like.'

I said, 'You can't do that when it's your first lover', and my mother frowned.

'I know,' said Lili, 'that's why it's vital to find a new one quickly.'

'They don't grow on trees,' said my mother, and I agreed with her silently.

'People always imagine they'll never love anyone else,' said Lili, 'like when you're freezing cold you can't imagine ever being warm again. We are silly creatures.'

I wanted to tell her that I was just such a silly creature and couldn't believe that I would ever be warm again.

Only once had I feared the heat of Egypt and that had

been in a waking dream. I had thought that I might ride in a *carretta* to the edge of the desert, and then walk away over the sand and into the sun. Sand was cleaner than water, the desert dead cleaner than the drowned dishevelled things which I had seen thrown up on shores. I had told myself that heat was cleansing, because I had grown fearful of water. Water, which I had loved, had become an agent of corruption. Perhaps only the sun could purify – burn me, burn the world into characterless dust. But dust lay all around me, a matter of constant irritation to Marie Claire, and the servants' principle task was fighting and dispersing it. I remembered that I too hated the dust, and as I imagined the walk into the desert I felt the sky come low and very close. There would be no room for the birds to fly, and dead birds would fall on me as I walked.

I had opened the louvered shutters and let in the real sun. The sun I had been dreaming of was dark, and the real sun was nothing: nothing but what it was.

Below, on the terrace, Marie Claire had heard me open the windows. 'Close them,' she had cried, 'you'll let in the dust', and I had gone down to drink *citron pressé* with her in the shade. That had not been long ago.

It was a lifetime ago.

*

My mother hadn't mentioned the matter of invitations for some days. She was waiting, hopelessly, for me to present her with a completed list and I wasn't going to. I saw my marriage as a kind of pointless secular martyrdom, but I baulked at putting brushwood around my own pyre.

'Right,' said my mother, holding a pen and a sheet of paper and looking nonchalant. 'Let's start on this list, shall we?'

Lili and Robert were out, and anyway there would have been no escape. I recited the names of some relations and friends, and my mother wrote them down in a businesslike fashion until I ran out of ideas.

'Marie Claire,' said my mother suddenly, beginning to write again.

After a while she looked up at me. 'Do think,' she said. 'We must have forgotten dozens of people.'

'Not Marie Claire,' I said.

'Don't be ridiculous,' protested my mother. 'You stayed with her for all that time. She's one of my oldest friends. Of course she must come. She may not be able to, but she must be asked.'

My mother and Marie Claire and Lili had all been at school together in Egypt. They had married in Egypt and been young matrons together. Marie Claire had married an Egyptian but since he was rich and cultured my mother hadn't minded and had continued with the friendship. They had sent each other Christmas cards. The fact that they had scarcely met for twenty years was immaterial and the bond between school fellows and fellow expatriates seemed stronger than ties of blood.

I dared not say any more, but my mother didn't mention Nour. She had never expressed much interest in Marie Claire's child. I suppose she had sent booties or a matinée jacket on the occasion of his birth, and sent him her love on the Christmas cards, but she didn't want to know what he was doing now. Marie Claire in her turn hadn't been interested in me. I thought that people were always disappointed in their old friends' children, seeing them as diluted, distorted versions of their parents, not nearly as much fun and full of peculiar new ideas. The fact that Lili seemed to take an interest in me led me to think that she had never been very close to my mother.

'Who was your best friend at school?' I asked.

My mother was surprised and undoubtedly gratified by this question.

'Well, Lili was first, then Marie Claire, then a German girl called Ilse ...'

She went on talking and I half-listened – just enough to be able to make a response when she stopped. If it didn't upset me too much I liked to make her happy. I wondered whether Lili would agree that they had been best friends. So I asked her.

'Oh yes, I think so,' said Lili, 'for a while. One's best friends kept changing.'

Everything kept changing. I hadn't known that this would happen. None of the people I knew had changed very much in my lifetime. My father had left, but everything apart from his absence was as it had been. To accept change took more courage than I possessed. All change was a forerunner of the last change. Death would come as a bridegroom and nothing then would ever be the same again. Yet I would prefer that contract. I would rather lose my self than share it with Syl. How inconvenient, I thought, that I should know that death was a suitor I could not seduce, that the choice of date lay only with him. No one could take death by force. It was my lot to live on the desert fringes where the rubbish lay.

My mother, wild with exasperation, one day again described me as a lump. I thought it an apt and correct description, with its connotations of inertia and lifelessness. She could just as well have been arranging my funeral for all the co-operation I offered her. I remembered what Lili had said about brides being gift-wrapped, and thought of them in their boxes. Dead people, like presents, were put into boxes. Brides were given away.

It didn't matter.

*

I began to think too often of the starveling cat. It had appeared in the garden of the villa one morning soon after Nour had returned for the holidays. I knew Nour was beautiful with the same sort of tutored, obedient awareness that led one to comprehend the merits of, say, the head of Nefertiti, but I didn't care. He meant no more to me than a painting or a sculpture. He wore nothing except shorts, and was unlike the head of Nefertiti in that he was self-conscious. I could see that he was pleased with himself, and yet I couldn't dislike him any more than I liked him. He was just there, with his long legs and his smooth shoulders and his golden hair and his pride.

I saw the little cat first. It crept towards the table where breakfast was laid, and it had the demeanour of a creature that wasn't loved and yet must survive. It was half-blind and its fur was staring and it expected nothing and desired nothing save the crust by the table leg on which its half-gaze was fixed.

There were mangoes on the table and flat bread and a dish of scrambled eggs, so I took a spoonful of egg and put it slowly down on the terrace, as I thought any human being would do. Then Nour turned and saw us, and he leapt from his chair and took a cup of coffee ready-poured and threw it at the cat, who was near my foot, so that my foot was covered in coffee and the cat fled. I said, 'No English boy would have done that.'

I sounded to myself absurd and thought he would laugh, but he said nothing except 'It's diseased', and he sat down again.

He was furious with me. It was an odd situation, since we didn't know each other well enough to be suddenly on such bad terms. Intimacy, I had learned, can begin in a strange variety of ways, and we now had a relationship where previously there had been nothing. And now again there was nothing. I was not loved yet must survive.

'What are you thinking about?' asked my mother.

'Nothing,' I said.

I was thinking about Nour and Marie Claire, and I was thinking about Syl and Mrs Monro. Each couple was like a parody of the other, their attitudes much the same. In some ways Syl and Nour were identical. It was like the sudden revelation of a pattern where none had been suspected, and I didn't at all care for it. I appeared twice like an ink blot on a folded sheet of paper: a passive, meaningless blur. I vowed to question Lili about predestination. It was, I felt sure, something about which she would have something to say.

She said she hadn't, but I don't think she was listening to me. She wanted to talk about Robert's exhibition. They were both out for most of the time, and my mother was torn between relief that they weren't under her feet all the time and resentment that they were treating her house like an hotel. Lili placated her with occasional presents marked with the stamp of central London – things from Soho, cheeses and *pâtés*, jam from Fortnum's, chocolates from Charbonnel et Walker. They made me think of beads and mirrors for the benighted natives.

'What do you find to do, out all day?' asked my mother, who only ventured out with a specific purpose in mind and always got back at the time she had decided she would. Lili's excursions, I felt, seemed to her gipsy-like in their apparent aimlessness, and vaguely immoral.

'Shows, exhibitions,' said Lili. 'Shops.'

My mother who did virtually nothing except cooking and the housework Mrs Raffald didn't do, and who went hardly anywhere, clearly considered this a terrible waste of time. She couldn't help disapproving of people. It seemed to be essential to her sense of identity, but I was finding it wearisome. So was Lili, who now proceeded to give us an account of the contents of the British Museum.

'Yes, I remember,' said my mother after a few minutes.

'Do you remember Old Ginger in the Egyptian room?' asked Lili.

'Yes,' said my mother. That was probably true since I, also, remembered Old Ginger. He had been curled up there, dead in his basket, since I had been a child in a velvet-collared coat.

'Morbid,' said my mother.

'And the winged beasts of the Babylonians,' said Lili. '*So wonderful*.'

My mother, who could have held nothing personal against these creatures, remarked that she had never liked them. She had got to the point where, if Lili had announced a passion for sun-kissed babies, she would have said she found them over-rated.

Lili relented, or perhaps she could think of no more artifacts to describe. I was almost certain that she had been to the British Museum no more recently than I had myself. I was almost certain that she spent the afternoons in a drinking club in Soho. She had never come home drunk. Nor had she ever come home footsore, as she surely must had she been quartering the city in the fashion she claimed. She smelt of the exhalations of other people's cigarettes and spilt wine, and she was expansive, with the air of someone who has spent time in the company of her like-minded fellows, not distracted and irritable as people are when they have tired themselves on the trail of trivial knowledge. She now set out to please my mother, not by pretence that she had been spending her time worthily, but in shared reminiscence.

This, as almost always, proved efficacious. My mother softened at once at the words 'Do you remember ...?' when they referred to her youth and not to her knowledge. There was no competition here, no assumed superiority on the part of another to make her uneasy or defensive, only what she saw as shared experience, delightful in retrospect. She seemed not to notice what I realised almost at once – that Lili's memory differed, not in essentials, but in flavour, from her own.

The Egypt of which they spoke was not the Egypt I had visited. It seemed to have been a place of school and tennis, of clubs and tennis. Of the people they spoke not at all. I wasn't surprised that my mother was silent on this subject – she acknowledged the existence of rather few people. Mrs Raffald was to her somehow unreal, a creature from another world; and foreigners, even in their own country, must have seemed infinitely remote. But Lili, I thought, should have known them, *must* have known them, for if she could see in me something to address then she could see something in any human being.

'The people were funny,' I said, as Lili stopped speaking, cigarette between her teeth, searching her pockets for her lighter.

'We have a sense of humour,' she agreed, unexpectedly becoming half-Egyptian as I watched.

The veiled women had reminded me of the nuns. They were much more like the nuns than were my fellow-countrywomen and co-religionists. Marie Claire was nothing like a nun and made a noise as she walked in her high-heeled shoes. The women, away from the men, used to laugh, and the nuns too were much more often merry than any European lay woman I could remember. I thought that the presence of men disinclined women from laughter and saw how Lili made my mother laugh as no man had ever done. My mother would often smile when speaking to men but dignity forbade hilarity in their presence. Or perhaps she simply didn't find them all that amusing. Once Nour had made me laugh, but then I had laughed – like the nuns

70

– more from happiness than mirth. I had laughed like the veiled women. Syl frequently made jokes, but I seldom smiled.

Mother Joseph, speaking her confident but imperfect Arabic, often had the beggars in stitches when they came to the convent gate for food. I had thought it a measure of their love and generosity that the nuns would make the suppliants laugh.

Marie Claire had been like my mother. She could speak to no one who would not have been admitted through the front door of her school.

Mother Joseph and the Mother of God, I thought, were quite unlike the mothers I knew. I wondered whether it was because neither of them had stirred herself to go through the contortions attendant upon attracting men, but it wasn't that. Nothing so simple. I decided that it was perhaps because they weren't possessive and had given no other human being the feeling that having been once disgorged he wasn't safe and at any moment might find himself gobbled up again and back in the confines of a body not his own. I thought, with revulsion, of my body in my mother's wedding dress.

I had drunk too much again. God was at the other end of the room. I thought perhaps he was smoking and reading. I knew he was there, but I couldn't see him and I thought he was unaware of me. Then I thought that he wasn't really there at all, and he wasn't God but my father, who also wasn't there. I had been abandoned. Now I can understand that isolation, but then I felt like the stray cat of Egypt, not only unloved but undeserving of all regard. And when my father came he wouldn't be the father whom I missed. The father I missed had never existed.

My mother had said to Lili one day that she thought I was marrying Syl because he was so much older than me

71

and would take the place of my father. Lili had said inconsequentially that Syl had been chasing young girls for years, and my mother had asked her crossly how she knew.

I was in the scullery washing mud off my shoes, still as I listened.

My mother hadn't denied Lili's assertion. She couldn't, for it was true. When I was a little girl and scarcely aware of Syl except as one of our neighbours, I had known that he was old to be unmarried and that the girls he brought home in his sports car were too young. It was a fact of life, like the tic in our milkman's left eye, and had meant no more to me. Lili had said, 'His mother told me.'

I wondered when Lili had seen Mrs Monro.

'Why should she do that?' my mother had asked scornfully, slapping something down on the kitchen table – a fish, I think.

I remember picturing the wet grease-proof paper it would be wrapped in and how my mother would cut off its head and scrape out its insides. There was nothing symbolic in my reflections – I didn't see my mother as a butcher of fish or of me. I just preferred to think of dead fish rather than Syl.

But Lili went on. 'Women are proud of their sons' prowess,' she said. 'She couldn't stand any of the girls, but she liked to think of Syl hauling them in. She said she used to get annoyed at the way he tired himself out running round after them, but she obviously thought it was jolly clever of him.'

'I can't imagine her telling you all that,' observed my mother. 'Why should she?'

'I asked her,' said Lili. 'I asked her why he wasn't married, and she didn't want me thinking there was anything wrong with him, so she told me. She says he likes looking after young people.

'There you are then,' said my mother. 'That's what I said.'

'The truth about chaps who want to be father figures,' remarked Lili, 'is that they actually want a mummy figure themselves. A little-known perversion.'

'Oh, fiddlesticks,' said my mother. 'He's got a mother already.'

'That makes no difference,' said Lili.

I had gone out into the garden, closing the scullery door as quietly as I could. Although I found it impossible to imagine such a conversation with Mrs Monro, I had no doubt that Lili was telling the truth, and whatever the psychological convolutions the facts were there. My mother had discovered that Syl sometimes disappeared in the night, was not at home when a respectable bachelor should be. She had sometimes called to find him absent and his mother's explanation, when she deigned to give one, unconvincing.

It had happened several times. The first time my mother had been indignant and remarked that Syl had no right to disappear for the evening without telling us where he was going. That had been when he had just engaged himself to me. I had said that her view was unreasonable and Syl was free to go out in the evening as he wished. 'Nonsense,' she had retorted. She had telephoned at nearly midnight to tell him I wasn't very well and he should call before office hours in the morning to cheer me up, but he wasn't back. I suspect that she may have telephoned yet again in the small hours. She said no more about it, but I knew she worried when these unexplained absences occured. The trouble was that Syl was usually expansive about his movements. He liked to tell anyone who would listen where he was going and what he was doing, and so my mother found his silences ominously strange. I thought he had probably

73

made an arrangement with a brothel-keeper, and sometimes I pictured him clinging to the branch of a tree peering in the darkness through the window of some schoolgirls' dormitory. Naturally he wouldn't wish to tell anyone where he was.

I had stood in the garden, and the wind, like a dressmaker, fitted my clothes to me, cold and indifferent. Stupid, I said to myself, stupid, stupid ... I spoke to myself and I didn't listen: meaningless words on deaf ears, although they were true, and whoever I was meant them, and whoever I was speaking to knew them for the truth. I wished I could turn to stone, or put down roots like the spotted laurel and forever let the adjusting wind tweak and fiddle with my clothes to no purpose.

Syl's previous engagement had ended only a few months before. I think it was his fourth, but as I had been a child during this proliferation of fiancées I wasn't certain. My mother undoubtedly had been counting, but she would have put the numbers out of her mind since they were evidence, at the very least, of instability on the part of her future son-in-law.

Syl didn't see it this way. He seemed to think it evidence of a malignant fate that he had had the misfortune to link himself to a succession of mad women. 'She was crazy,' he said of the last reneging fiancée when he first turned his attention to me. 'She used to burst into tears when we were having our happiest times.' She had tried to get out of the car when he was driving and he considered it lucky that they hadn't been killed, but as he and I were together more I came to admire her resolution and good sense. She had been as insignificant in appearance as all the other girls I had seen him with: as insignificant as I was myself. I wondered whether he eschewed beautiful women because he feared competition from them, or from other men.

'She was always arguing,' said Syl, sounding bewildered. I felt then that I understood her. If I hadn't been weak and without hope I should have quarrelled with almost everything Syl said. If I had been brave I would have hit him. He was, I think, even more solipsistic than I was: self-centred as only a man constrained within his own view of what constituted his masculinity could be. I wasn't trapped within a vision of my femaleness. I had no consciousness of it. I saw that despite his good looks Syl was a little too short and a little too fat, that when he went about his garden stripped to bathing trunks he aroused not desire but embarrassment. I was too miserable to giggle, but I wondered if the fiancées had when he postured on his lawn. Even his kindness was repellent. One day he put his hand on mine and said he wanted me to be happy, and distaste, or perhaps anger, made me cruel. I knew he was convinced that if he made love to me I should be happy. He had frequently said as much.

'You're like my mother,' I said. 'You're exactly like my mother. You sound like her and you even look like her.'

But he only listened interestedly because whatever I was saying I was talking about him.

'You're womanly,' I said. 'You behave like a woman, running round looking after people. That's why your girls ran away from you. Because you ran after them, flapping like a woman.'

I had no wish to marry anyone now that I couldn't marry Nour, but I was particularly averse to the idea of marrying my mother. I didn't say so, because the idea was too unpleasant to be clothed in words and made visible.

I said again I didn't love him, but he didn't believe me.

He went on listening, not saying a word.

'You're babyish too,' I said. 'You're a baby with your car and your games.'

He still listened, but now I don't think he was hearing me, not believing that I meant what I said. There was something so wrong between us that he grew instantly fonder of me, and oddly enough I didn't mind the rest of the evening we spent together. He seemed less absurd, more mature, and I don't know why. I know he paid no attention to my words. Perhaps, because I had really addressed myself to him for the first time, he thought we were in accord. I wondered then whether when two people speak together they ever really hear anything but what they say themselves, and what they wish to hear from the other.

I seldom speak now. There is no need for speech. Perhaps there never was.

*

Events that seemed to me to lie in a past as remote as the Second Kingdom were as vivid now to my mother and Lili as the day they had happened. They both remembered a party at the Yacht Club in Alexandria that had taken place fifteen years before: the food, the people, the clothes. My mother remembered the food and some of the people, and Lili remembered different people and the clothes.

'There was style then,' she said. 'How old that makes me sound.'

She got up and looked in the alcove mirror.

'I, of course, still have it,' she remarked, 'and I always will, only everyone else has lost it. How unfortunate for them.'

I saw perfect truth in this, and even my mother didn't trouble to deny it.

'The King was there,' Lili said.

'He wasn't,' said my mother, perhaps because she had concurred for too long and now it was time for contradiction.

'I danced with him,' said Lili. 'I was wearing lime-green

chiffon and my mother's emeralds. He was a nice king. My father loved him. The people loved him.'

I had taken no interest in Egyptian politics, but this struck me as a novel view. My mother was, I think, almost as ignorant on the subject as I was myself, having lived only in the nutshell of the English enclave, and she was silent.

'He didn't stay long,' said Lili in a comforting tone. 'He was a very busy king. Do you remember? We walked home, along the Corniche and all the way back to Camp Caesar.'

'I didn't,' said my mother. 'You wouldn't have caught me walking the streets in my dancing shoes.'

'I remember you,' said Lili. 'You had a little cream velvet coat with feather trimmings round the sleeves.'

'I remember *that*,' said my mother, 'but I went home in the Embassy car.'

'We went past a house where there'd been a wedding,' said Lili, 'the night before. We walked past in the dawn and there, hanging from the window, was the bride's nightdress, all bloodstained.'

'Why on earth ...?' said my mother, who knew less of the native customs than she did of their politics. 'Had he killed her?'

She looked alarmed, and even though I knew the significance of this rite, because Nour had told me, for a moment I shared her confusion, her small anxiety at the thought of the violence of that long-past nuptial night.

'No, of course he hadn't killed her,' said Lili impatiently. 'He'd have killed her if there hadn't been any blood. They'd all have killed her. Her own family first. They'd have lapidated her. Put her in a hole and stoned her and covered her up with earth before she was dead. And then forgotten all about her – even her name.'

My mother thought about this for a moment until comprehension came to her, whereupon she changed the subject out of deference to my youth and inexperience.

'What was the name of that chef?' she asked. 'The French one. The one who would go round to all the different clubs and people's houses and do the cooking there. Pierre? Jacques? Jean ...? He was wonderful with fish.'

'I don't remember him,' said Lili. 'I prefered Egyptian food in those days – *baba ganouche* and ...'

'Oh, I know,' said my mother laughing crossly. '*Foul medames*, I suppose.'

'You pronounce it "fool",' said Lili placidly, 'as you very well know.'

'I know you used to drag me to native cafés,' said my mother. 'I used to think I'd die of cholera on the spot.'

'You never ate the salad,' said Lili. 'You don't know what you were missing.'

I couldn't visualise my mother in one of the Arab cafes. I just couldn't. 'Where was I?' I asked, with dim, disjointed childish memories of dark, blinded rooms and sudden blinding sunlight overlaid by newer memories of similar rooms and the same sunlight.

'You were usually with me,' said my mother virtuously. 'Or with Nanny in the villa garden.'

Now that Lili was here my lifelong image of her had become confused. She had leaned forward on the grassy bank and she was speaking and I couldn't remember what she was saying. I wished I could, for I couldn't forget that what she had said had seemed significant, and of greater, stronger import than anything she had said since she had come back. I wondered where the grassy bank had been. In the villa garden? Or had we travelled out to one of the villages? It seemed unlikely.

'Another drink,' said Lili. '*Emfadlek.*'

I forgot their talk of parties and food and clothes and felt the unknown bride's nightdress around me, wet with blood, marked by change. Again I saw change as the enemy. I had heard my mother's friends sometimes whispering ruefully of The Change, but I saw the loss of innocence as the greatest and the worst change. Once accomplished it left one spoiled for ever and forever incomplete, all integrity gone. It was nothing to do with morality, I was thinking. It was more to do with the jars of jam on the pantry shelves. Once opened they were as good as finished. I knew what Syl would say if I tried to explain my thoughts to him, because Nour had said it already. He would say that it was the purpose and blissful destiny of a pot of jam to be opened and eaten up. To give pleasure and be obediently laid on bread was its *raison d'etrê*. Jam left in the jar, he would say, would turn bitter and go off and be of no use to anyone. Nour had said it all, although of course he hadn't spoken in terms of jam, but more directly. His words hadn't affected me at all. I had been lost because I loved him. There was, I thought, something shoddy, pathetic and defeated about an opened jar of jam. How much more pleasing to the eye and the higher senses were the gleaming unbroached jars in the pantry, and how I suddenly hated the men who had assured me that in their attentions lay my fulfilment. I wished for the first time that I had taken that knife and turned it on Nour and let *his* blood.

Then Lili said, 'I must go up and change.' And I laughed.

I soon stopped, since as far as my mother knew there was nothing to laugh at and she was looking at me. Inexplicable laughter would, I was sure, seem to my mother yet another of the first signs of madness.

*

Lili came down again in a black jersey frock and fresh lipstick and carrying the scent of some strange perfume.

'That takes me back,' exclaimed my mother. 'Now that really does take me back. It's that dreadful stuff you got in the bazaars.'

'I like it,' said Lili, 'though I wouldn't wear it every day. Just for a change.'

'It's overpowering,' said my mother, fanning her nose with her hand.

'It is *verree erotique*,' said Lili, affecting a foreign accent. 'It *is*, actually,' she went on in a normal voice. 'It drives men wild. Even camel drivers, and you wouldn't think they'd notice.'

'Nobody could fail to notice it,' said my mother.

'Derek used to like it,' said Lili. She stood lighting a cigarette and looking at my mother out of the corners of her eyes.

My mother was again plunged into a version of that dilemma common to all divorced wives. Either she could say that Derek was the biggest fool the world had ever seen – in which case she would stand, self-confessed, as an even bigger fool for having married him in the first place. Or she could say that Derek had always had charming manners and was in the habit of commending ladies on their scent, even if it smelled of Alexandrian sewers, and sound as though she had lost something worth keeping – and inevitably regretful. Or she could, if she thought of it in time, say that Derek had always been the most frightful liar.

We watched her, Lili interestedly and I apprehensively.

'Derek had very little sense of smell,' said my mother.

Lili was kind. 'You're quite right,' she said. 'He never complained like the rest of you when it was really hot.'

She had said 'the rest of you' and I had never heard her

so distance herself before, but what astonished me was the realisation that my father must have been at that party, must have returned with my mother to the villa in the small hours, must have been aware of me in my little white pyjamas and Panama hat. My mother had several photographs of me in this attire. She said, with satisfaction, that she had never made the mistake of the other English wives and forced me into liberty bodices and starched frocks. Yet I remembered a pale-green crêpe dress with rosebuds on it that was too tight under the arms and prickly round the neck, and a navy-blue sailor suit with a white collar that chafed. I remembered wearing English sandals and white socks, and a white lambswool cardigan for the cool of the evening and lawn nightdresses and winceyette knickers, aertex shirts and grey-flannel shorts. I remembered all sorts of things and my young father hardly at all. There had been an office somewhere near the Corniche: tall rooms with charts on the walls, Arab coffee in tiny cups, secretaries smiling, silent ... But the glimpse of memory had gone and I was furnishing the room from later experience. Marie Claire had friends with similar offices.

My mother said with patient scorn, 'Speaking of Derek, we'd better ring him and make sure he hasn't forgotten about the wedding.'

I said, 'Cynthia wouldn't let him', which was silly of me because it aroused several emotions in my mother.

I think what had happened to my father was this. He had been married to my mother for fifteen years and had been called a bad husband, whereas she had been what is known as a good wife. That is, she had been faithful, and domineering, and had demanded proper behaviour of him. Under her crumpled linen skirts had been concealed the pants. Since she had begun by taking charge he had let her continue doing so, and had responded by being more feckless, lazier and more contrary than he was by nature. A marriage only needs, can only support, one strong partner, and my mother had claimed that role for herself. When my father tired of the pretence involved in this relationship (for he wasn't as weak as they had tacitly agreed) he had hastened to the other extreme and married a woman who, as my mother was fond of remarking, you could pour into a jug.

Cynthia was given to what used to be known as the 'vapours'. She would call my father home from his place of work because there was a spider in the sink. She wept if the milkman seemed disrespectful. She had refused to breast-feed her two children because she thought it disgusting, and my father in middle age had spent many wakeful nights, not cavorting in the pleasure grounds of a foreign city, but walking the floor feeding his children from a bottle while his new wife lay in a sedative-induced slumber. My mother couldn't understand it, but her rage and jealousy had long since given way to contempt and the occasional satisfaction of genuine sympathy. I wouldn't have changed places with my father's new children who, although they were five and seven, still seemed to smell of damp nappies and regurgitated milk, but I used sometimes to wonder what I would have been like if he had devoted similar time to me and not left me entirely to the women.

'Cynthia wouldn't let him, indeed,' my mother repeated after me, italicising her words. 'Huh,' she said.

But I knew that Cynthia liked weddings and parties and dances. At least she said she did. I didn't see her often, but whenever we met she would complain gently that they never went anywhere because Derek was always so busy or the babbas were teething or undergoing the whooping cough. And when, by good fortune, they had contrived to attend some glittering function Cynthia would delight in describing it, with especial reference to the people she had met, the important positions they occupied, and the deep respect in which they held her husband. She was a desperately tiresome female, but I always felt constrained to be pleasant to her merely because she was so uninspiring. I had wondered once whether that was the reason my father had married her, but that was before I had learned that men are not much given to acts of altruism, and certainly not in sexual matters. Improbable as it was, he must have been in love with her. She had been nineteen like me, and youth, as I knew, even when its possessor is unattractive, has an appeal of its own. She was still young, but her teeth stuck out. Perhaps one day my father would leave her too. He gave little appearance of being unusually happy. On the other hand he wasn't particularly sad. Not as I knew sadness. Perhaps, after all, anguish died with time, and life became a simple matter of bills and procreation and sometimes going to parties. The prospect didn't give me new heart, offering as it did yet another barren dimension to the future with Syl. It wasn't that I thought myself deserving of more delight than was offered the mass of mankind (I told myself) but that the common lot seemed so dire. I wouldn't let myself think how I had hoped to marry Nour and the happiness I had anticipated. Incredulity at my own stupidity almost made me laugh, for Nour would, without a shadow of a doubt, have many, many wives and not one of them would ever be happy.

*

Lili and my mother were still remembering. They were talking of Mr Monro, who had died, it seems, of whisky and soda many years before: before I was born. They spoke of

83

him as 'Syl's father' and I thought that death, like marriage, depersonalised people. Now he was dead he was no longer Jack Monro but only Syl's father, the dead husband of Mrs Monro, and soon I would be Margaret Monro. Everything was a reflection of death, not only birth but marriage.

'I brought you a bottle of gin,' said Lili.

I got up quickly and fetched three glasses. Too quickly, for my mother looked at me as I put them on the table. She would have liked to deny me the gin and vermouth I was craving, but I would soon be a married woman and she couldn't. The vermouth was dark red, and I wondered what my mother would do if I poured it on the mushroom-coloured carpet – very slowly. That would not be the action of a responsible woman on the eve of her wedding. Perhaps she would cancel the wedding, would say to Syl, 'You cannot marry my daughter. She has poured vermouth on my carpet and is not a fit person to wed.' But Syl would be angry. I had seen him angry. He hated to be thwarted and went white with rage when his car wouldn't start. Once he had taken me to Brighton for the day. I had said I didn't want to go, that I was tired and that I didn't like the sea. I meant the people who gather by the sea and the noise and the colours and the smell of frying, but Syl had gone pale and sworn at me, using a word I had never been called before, and saying only a moron would say she didn't like the sea. I had to agree with him. But how could I explain to a man shaking with fury that it was candy-floss I didn't like, and crowds, and being with him?

One of Syl's ways of expressing displeasure was by tightening the purse strings. He was naturally mean but aware that this was an unattractive characteristic; therefore he was always swift to take an opportunity of indulging his parsimony with a clear conscience. When I annoyed him he

84

would punish me by economising on whatever it was we were doing at the time. Should I express a taste for wine he would order half a bottle, or sometimes say outright that it was bad for me and I should drink lemonade. He would drink lemonade himself if he was sufficiently offended, and then add to my other transgressions the blame for spoiling his outing by denying him wine. Today he walked past the expensive fish restaurant where he had planned to lunch and into a steam-clouded fish-and-chip shop.

We had driven in silence and walked in silence and eaten fish in silence. I had wondered how a man in his right mind could want to be with me and decided that no girl in her right mind would want to be with him. I was the only one he could control. I was afraid of him.

'Syl's late,' remarked my mother. 'He said he'd call in on the way home.' She spoke to Syl more than I did. They seldom had a conversation but they arranged things together: things like my life. I poured myself more of the sweet red vermouth.

'Don't drink too much of that,' said my mother, unable to stop herself; but it made me feel better, more like the early girl of Egypt and less like the starveling cat.

*

Syl and Robert arrived at the same time and my mother poured them drinks. They talked about Robert's exhibition, and to an outsider the scene would have appeared normal: a group of friends in an English house on an English evening. I don't remember much of it. The last I remember thinking was that Syl should marry my mother, his contemporary, and that then perhaps I would have to call him Daddy. I must have smiled, because Syl smiled back at me and leaned across and took my hand. My

85

mother had looked cheerful and I had gone to bed seeing her cheerful face.

I had drunk too much and woke in the night knowing I was damned. There is nothing to do about being damned. I lay in the darkness but my soul lay, the insect's child, washed in endless light. Light made me powerless. In the dark I could manoeuvre, hide in the alleys of incomprehension, crouch behind the walls of indifference, know that I existed, and hope because I couldn't be seen. Only perfection can flower in the light. It is eternal and it illuminates despair. Hell is the absence of God, the absence even of his shadow. Much grief, much pain is experienced in the shadow of God, but despair comes where he is not. You can pray, you can say the words, but there is no communion, and you cannot close your eyes.

I sat up and turned on the bedside light to see the shadows in the room. There was really nothing else I could do. I had been party to a murder, and I didn't care.

*

Robert's exhibition was the next highlight in our lives. We went in Syl's car, his mother and mine in the back and me in the place of honour beside Syl. I felt childish and rebellious and irrelevant to all that was happening.

The gallery was full and the gallery owner looked happier than when I had last seen him. Already there were red stars on some of the pictures. I saw Robert and I saw Lili. They looked odd to me. It was as though Robert had given birth and Lili was handing out cigars. He wore a pleased but modest look and Lili looked as though she knew she was expected to appear proud. I thought she was proud but aware that she should be prouder. This made me uneasy, and I was glad when someone gave me a glass of white wine.

I was caught in a group near the door and it took me some

time to realise that I ought to be looking at the pictures, since that was why we were there. They seemed to be mostly line-and-wash with an occasional burst of colour, and even when I got close to them I found I had to concentrate to see what they were about.

Not for too long, though. I immediately recognised the subject of the third picture I looked at. It was of the gate to Marie Claire's villa: a clear bold drawing of the tall wrought-iron gate I had watched the girl go through on the first night I saw her. One of the scrolls was broken. I had always put my hand on that attenuated strip of iron to push the gate open.

*

She had appeared one evening at the kitchen door with her hands outstretched, though not very far. She wasn't like the other beggars, not quite a supplicant; fairer than the maids and with her head uncovered. I was sitting under a tree in the evening coolness and I watched her. Both maids came out, and although there were only two of them they seemed to surround and overwhelm her, not threateningly, but eagerly as though she brought gifts. They spoke in Arabic, but I thought they didn't understand each other very well. Her voice was harsh and she gestured with her outstretched hands. The maids laughed as they did when they were alone and they brought her bread and half a roasted pigeon. She sat on the ground and ate them while the maids watched in the fading light. I could smell the citronella that I put on my skin to ward off the mosquitoes and feel the breeze beginning to rise from the river. Fatima brought out an oil lamp and sat beside her. She stopped eating and threw the bones of the pigeon away. Secretly the maids used to leave food in hidden corners for the dogs, but not

87

when Marie Claire was around. Marie Claire held that this practice encouraged rats and snakes, but the maids thought Allah smiled upon their benevolence. At least I think that's what they thought. Like the nuns they never refused a beggar and, no matter what Marie Claire's opinions of that were, there was nothing she could do to prevent them.

The girl stretched out a hand and took a fold of Fatima's dress between her fingers. She sat still, and I believe her eyes were closed. Nobody could sit so still with her eyes open. After a while she began to speak again and Fatima listened, her elbows on her knees and her chin on her hands. There was something enthralling about this scene, the three girls in the circle of insect-laden light, so that I hadn't wondered what she was doing and only now did I realise that the girl was a fortune-teller. She spoke – more slowly than she had spoken before – and Fatima listened with a concentrated intensity that she never lent to Marie Claire's requests and detailed instructions. It was evident in all their dealings that no matter how Marie Claire bestirred herself the maids would do things as they had always done them. Now, watching her, I thought that Fatima might, at this girl's behest, change her life, her ways, and I wondered what she would do if she was hearing that she would find no husband, have no children, lose her life to Leviathan. What if the fortune-teller was destroying her hope and joy with that strange, harsh voice. But Fatima was laughing and loving herself with crossed arms. The husband, I thought, was assured, and the many fine sons. The fortune-teller would hardly relay bad tidings, for who would be generous, learning of coming sorrows? Hala took Fatima's place and the girl reached out and plucked a pin from the scarf which concealed her hair. Hala giggled and rocked back and forth and Fatima moved closer to watch. They were full of movement, the maids, but the strange girl was as still as a

88

hunting cat, her fingers closed over the cheap pin and her eyes open now. I saw them gleam in the lamp-light. Hala was little and round and fat like a quail, and the girl, like a cat, stared at her in unblinking silence. I thought I should clap my hands and shatter the scene, send the cat leaping into the bushes where the snakes lay coiled, send the quail flapping into the house and safety. I no longer thought the fortune-teller would foretell only good things, for the girl had a cruel face.

Marie Claire called from the balcony. Supper was late. Nour came into the garden. The maids skipped into the kitchen. The girl slipped away, not to the bushes but out through the curled iron gates to the earth lane that bordered the river.

*

Somebody said, 'Can I give you more wine?'

I said, 'No.' There might be crocodiles in it.

*

I heard Ahmed, the porter, boasting to Marie Claire in the heat of the following morning. He had come as he did each day with bread from the baker's iron oven that stood open to the lane in the souk. I felt hotter than I need have done as I thought of the man who fed the dough on long, long shovels into that blazing hole. Once Nour had said to me, 'Margaret, would you like to be that man, burning all your life, or would you rather marry me?'

His mother had made him take me out to see the sights and he was bored and resentful. He would lead me through small flocks of goats, or to where the traffic was worst, and then briefly hide from me in the narrow alley-ways or the open shops. 'I would sooner swim in the pool with the crocodiles than marry you,' I had said. I wasn't brave then; I was never brave, but I was not yet broken.

Ahmed had come from that dizzy town to boast that he had seen a bad strange girl leaving Marie Claire's house and had shouted and thrown stones at her. He boasted in French, but I understood him. He should have seemed ridiculous, the big man, demonstrating how he had put a girl to flight, but I felt sorry for him. I believed that a murrain would fall on the hens that he kept on his house-top, a wasting illness on the sheep that he kept by his door. I feared for the health of his mother and the aunts who lived with him. I wondered about the future of his wife and his little children. I thought that perhaps I would sooner have swum in the pool with the crocodiles than draw to myself the hostile attention of that girl.

I called, '*Ahmed, elle est mauvaise, cette fille.*'

He turned to me, smiling with his few teeth.

'*Mais oui,*' he said, and I shrugged in the sunlight, trying to disregard the foreign mists of foreboding. It was nothing to do with me if the porter wished to bring himself to the notice of Shaitan. I said to myself, Don't be stupid, Margaret, for my religion forbade superstition, and I sipped bitter black coffee.

'Which girl is bad?' asked Nour, his hair dark gold from the wetting of the shower, and I felt I would rather swim in the pool with the crocodiles than tell him about the girl like a cat. Perhaps I had always been in love with him.

'The peasant,' said Ahmed in English, 'who troubled the house last night. She is a bad girl.'

'I saw her,' said Nour, and I looked away.

'Pretty,' said Nour, and the cup I was holding shook.

'Nour,' said Marie Claire, giving him the warning glance that only a mother can command.

'*Ooh la la*,' said Nour, looking up to smile directly at me with the triumph of the creature who knows himself to be irresistible.

When he saw my face he stopped smiling and his eyelids lowered. I had given myself away. I had bestowed myself on Nour, and from now on he could do with me as he would. I knew what he was thinking, as I watched him realising this. For a while it made him like me.

He reached over to touch my wrist, and his look was tender. I was more surprised than gratified, for without having really considered it I would have expected unsolicited adoration to annoy Nour, to lead to stone-throwing …

*

It was as though I had slept and had dreamed. I awoke to find myself still standing before the water-colour painting of the curled iron gate. I could almost feel the river running behind me, beyond the earthen path.

'Like it?' asked Lili. 'Have some more wine.'

'It's Marie Claire's gate,' I said.

'Do you think so?' asked Lili, her head tilted. 'I don't think so. It's just a typical villa gate.' She wandered away, bottle in one hand, cigarette in the other.

I stared at the opposite wall. Robert had used pastels to draw a group of earthenware pots and jugs.

'That's nice,' I said to a stranger, speaking only to reassure myself that I could.

He didn't answer. It was a pleasing picture. I looked at it for a long time until Marie Claire's kitchen began to form itself around the pots.

Syl was trying with kindling glances and *doubles entendres* to enthral the girl who worked in the gallery. I couldn't hear what he was saying, but I didn't need to. I had heard it all before and could only think how differently she would be responding if Syl had been Nour. She looked puzzled and rather angry, and Syl looked old and silly. He saw me watching him and leaned forward to touch the girl on the shoulder, and then came towards me.

I turned and pushed my way through a group of people to the end of the room. It was unbearable that the gallery girl should imagine that I belonged to Syl, that his glances and suggestive remarks had ensnared me. I forgot that sometimes he could be quiet and kind, and I hated him. I stared at a picture of a cedar tree in curious perspective. The paintings seemed to bear the same relation to reality as prayers to the vision of God. In a word I found them inadequate, not to say hopeless. Perhaps vision can never be recaptured or reconstituted. Perhaps there are no words or pigments capable of carrying meaning, and all our flourishes are a waste of time.

Lili was talking to someone behind me. 'Being the object of many men's desire,' she was saying authoritatively, 'makes one feel like a bus.'

I thought she must at least be a little drunk, for it seemed an odd remark for even Lili to make to a stranger, but the stranger said, 'What can you mean, Lili?' So she wasn't a stranger but a friend: one of the friends of Lili's London afternoons; a woman dressed in black wool with silver hoop earrings.

'Your average whore,' explained Lili clearly, 'goes round like a taxi cab touting for trade, but the innocent irresistible woman is like a municipal bus. It isn't her fault that people keep running after her, and it's unpleasant for her, people jumping on and off ...'

Somebody pushed between us and I could no longer hear what she was saying.

Few people were talking about Robert's paintings. The ones who were looking at them were looking silently and glancing at their catalogues, and the rest were talking about other matters — mostly about where they had last met. I moved along past the drawings to look at a blurred water-colour with a wild smudge of cobalt in the centre. The blue, after a while, revealed itself as the dress of a woman walking behind an ox. This painting was larger than the others and more like everybody else's Egypt, the Egypt the traveller expected. There were date palms in the middle ground and I shouldn't have been surprised to see a pyramid in the distance.

This was a little reassuring. To find a country unlike your imaginings of it, and then to find a series of representations by somebody else of your own experience, gives a sense of intrusion. I felt as though Robert had used my eyes.

'The assumption is that women like to be desired by many men.' I could hear Lili again as the crowd shifted. 'A wrong assumption,' she said, 'as any woman in that situation will tell you — if, that is, she has the wit to recognise her reactions. Many people don't ...'

I heard Syl's voice saying, 'Oh, come on, Lili', and I moved further away, not wishing to hear his opinion. I thought it likely that an unruly argument would develop between them, with Syl insisting that no woman could get enough admiration and Lili denying it. Lili could be difficult, and Syl was irredeemably convinced that men were the principal object of every woman's thoughts.

The next picture I looked at was of Marie Claire's bedroom. Marie Claire was in it, her back to the viewer, her hair down, naked. The gilded chair by the dressing-table was strewn with clothing, just as I had seen it when I had sometimes taken in her morning *tisane*. I told myself it could be any bedroom, and the woman any woman, but even in Robert's blurred, shadowy style it was unmistakable, and Marie Claire's back recognisable. I thought that this was a painting I shouldn't discuss with Lili, but only when I had walked to the end of the gallery to look at an innocuous picture of a group of long-haired sheep did I ask myself what Robert had been doing in Marie Claire's bedroom.

I should have stopped looking at the pictures then, when past and present had clashed in my mind and made no meaning, but I went on. Some of the scenes were unfamiliar, though not many. Again and again I recognised vistas, buildings, details of tree and ditch. He had even painted the convent where I had sought consolation in my early homesickness and had agreed with Mother Joseph that I should apply to the Mother House to be accepted as a postulant and return in the course of time, if God so willed, as a professed nun to help her teach the children and grow the herbs and milk the goats and say the prayers in the cool chapel. I looked at Robert's painting, reflecting how I had spoiled my life: a life that I had muddied and bloodied and ruined.

I looked for respite at the catalogue. None of the places was named. The paintings had silly names like 'Gateway' and 'Woman in Blue' and 'Vespers'. I thought that Robert had covered his tracks well and then that it was inconceivable that Lili, who knew everything, shouldn't have known all that her husband did.

I came to a picture called 'Crocodile Pool'. I don't know how long I stood in front of it.

'Like that one, do you?' Syl was behind me, his hands on my shoulders.

'Lovely,' I said, as lifeless as the painted image. It was a good picture, if, I told myself, you liked that sort of thing. There were no figures in it. None of the villagers would go near the pool, which was what made it such a suitable place for a rendezvous. There was an old broken mud house nearby with a fallen tower where the pigeons had lived, and trees like willows hanging over the still water.

'None of the villagers would go near it,' said Lili beside me. 'They said it was full of crocodiles, but that was nonsense. There hasn't been a crocodile there for donkeys' ages. It's haunted by some awful phantom, or a devil or something. Robert had a terrible time painting it. People kept waving warnings at him from a distance.'

'How do *you* know?' asked Robert. 'You weren't there.'

'You told me,' said Lili.

I turned to look at her face and saw her smiling.

'You said they were always yelling at you from the fields, and brandishing sticks.'

Her smile seemed to me to be defiant and triumphant and accepting all at once, which was ridiculous since a smile is only a smile: sometimes honest, sometimes forced – no more. I was reading into it what I thought she must be feeling, certain that she wasn't threatened by Robert's infidelity, yet challenging him with her smile. Robert seemed unnaturally unperturbed.

I wondered what he would say if I should remark that just outside the right-hand frame there lay a disused water wheel, and that the low wall of the ruined house had a hollow place where it was comfortable to sit, shaded by what remained of the pigeon tower. I knew that he too would tell me I was wrong and that it was in another part of the country. Perhaps he would be speaking the truth and this small scene was repeated the length of the Nile.

'They kept finding bodies in it,' he said.

*

95

It was agreed the next day that I was run down. It was also agreed that the gallery had been overheated and airless and that I had drunk too much. I had held on to Lili, and Syl had brought me home insisting that our mothers should stay and go on to dinner with Lili and Robert and the gallery owner as planned. I remember looking into Mrs Monro's face and seeing that she looked concerned, and being surprised.

My own mother looked cross. Syl, too, was angry with me. It seemed that he wouldn't be kind when I was ill, but only when I was badly behaved and unpleasant to him. That night I felt too sick to be any such thing. He took me to my room but didn't offer to help me further. This was fortunate, for if he had touched me I think I would have gone mad.

Later in the day it was agreed that the honeymoon trip to Egypt should be cancelled. I wondered whether I had said something that I couldn't remember, perhaps had shrieked or whispered that I wouldn't go back, but Lili said she had heard it was unusually hot for the time of year and unsuitable for a run-down person. My mother argued for a while that the dry heat was known to be bracing, but Lili went on to speak of rumours of a cholera epidemic in the rural districts and disaffection among the *fellahin* and I said I would rather go to Bournemouth, which was a black lie but efficacious since we had gone there for our holidays and my mother seemed gratified that I should wish to return. Syl however was angry again. It appeared that he would lose money by this cancellation and despite his liking for the seaside he didn't want to go to Bournemouth.

Scotland, suggested my mother, and Syl said at least he would be able to get in some shooting, but I don't think he ever did anything about it. Already it seemed that the wedding was to be an ending and nothing lay beyond it but a prospect as vague and as shadowy as one of Robert's landscapes. It contrasted unfavourably with the structured clarity of the convent.

A little fat nun had once cried in the heat of Egypt's afternoon, in the accents of County Cork, that she wished she could take off her flesh and sit by the well in her bones. I day-dreamed that I could do the same and we would sit together unashamed in the afternoon sun. I could hear the click of rosary beads on bone and an Irish voice saying, '*Ave Maria, gratia plena* ...' And behind it another voice, '*Ora pro nobis* ...' That was mine. My soul breathed between my bones, and my flesh was an encumbrance.

'Margaret.'

I looked up. There was no ease among the people in the room. I had for too long been conscious only of my own concerns, but now I became aware that those around me were troubled and at odds. With the egocentricity of all human creatures, exacerbated by my youth and misery I assumed that I was the cause and source of this lack of comfort and stirred myself to attempt to dispel it.

I said humbly, 'I hope I didn't spoil the evening.'

'Oh no,' said my mother sarcastically.

'Not *you*,' said Robert.

I stared at him because he sounded so cold, but he was sitting looking down at the glass which he held on his knees and I couldn't see his face.

I glanced at Lili thinking that she must know and would somehow reveal what was disturbing him. I still thought of them as indissoluble despite the picture of Marie Claire's bedroom. On one level I knew that Robert had been unfaithful to Lili and on another I knew that he couldn't possibly have been. I found no difficulty at all in believing both these things, having been forced to extend my capacity for credibility to accommodate stranger and more terrible

97

inconsistencies. Lili looked calm and showed no sign of the guilt she must surely have felt had Robert meant his words as an accusation against her. But whom else could he be blaming? And for what?

I asked doubtfully, 'Was the exhibition a success?'

'Oh yes,' said Lili.

My mother spoke suddenly. It seemed to me that the question she asked had been simmering in her for some time. 'How do you know,' she said, 'when you left so early?'

She sounded ill-tempered and I realised that in the absence of me, Syl *and* Lili she must have dined alone with Mrs Monro and Robert and the gallery owner. It was, I thought, a measure of her self-control that she had waited until now to express her annoyance.

'It was a success from the very beginning,' said Lili.

I thought I heard her say that she'd packed the gallery, but she was lighting a cigarette and no one took any notice of this remark.

'I was tired,' she added without apology. 'I just came home, let myself in by the back door and went straight to bed.'

She had done no such thing. I had lain awake the better part of the night. My room was over the back door and it squeaked like a murdered rat. I had heard my mother and Robert come in and had gone to sleep much later. If Lili had come in by the back door it had been very late indeed.

Robert yawned and said nothing.

'We couldn't think where you were,' said my mother, 'we hunted for you for hours.'

'Oh sorry,' said Lili. 'Sorry, sorry.'

Syl left soon after that. It was Sunday the next day and he would be playing golf.

'You mustn't lose any more beauty sleep,' said Lili, and I thought she spoke to me. I felt foolish for having mentioned the exhibition and caused the display of ill-temper. I should have kept quiet and remained as the focus of disapproval.

*

When I went to bed it was as though the night was last night and no day had come to separate them.

I had tried not to remember, but Robert's paintings made forgetfulness impossible. Even if I had no longer been able to see the real images in my mind I could see their representations as clearly as if they hung before me, and the two were beginning to run together. I could almost hear voices. '...see where the water moves...' '...the wind...' '...no wind from the Nile, there is never a wind from the Nile...' '...there is, there must be...' '...Herodotus...' '...who?..' '...Herodotus said there is never a wind from the Nile, never, never...' Nour had laughed because I had not heard of Herodotus. We were in competition: competition of sex, of race. Nour drew me as an English Miss: Ingleesy, prim, uneducated, unsophisticated. I set him as a foreigner: untrustworthy, slyly clever, un-English. We were both entirely correct in our estimations of each other, only there was, as there always is, more to it than that.

'Once upon a time,' I said, 'people believed that horse-hair grew into eels.'

'Stupid girl,' said Nour, bored with me. He was sitting on the wall by the broken tower where the pigeons had lived.

'And they thought barnacles turned into geese,' I said, racking my brains for ancient nonsense.

Nour laughed again. 'Dirty girl,' he said.

I stared at him.

'Geese is Arabic for fart,' he told me.

I had never heard the word and unwisely said that I didn't know what it meant. Nour told me that too. I was more shocked than embarrassed and didn't blush. Where I came from no one spoke of such things. He was disappointed at my failure to react and puzzled. I had been at great pains to appear distant towards him and been more successful than I had thought I could be. Nour was beginning to doubt the evidence of his senses.

'How vulgar,' I said, not turning my face from him.

It was Nour who looked away.

'And what, pray, is the Arabic for those long-necked water birds?' I asked. I had never teased anyone before, but I felt a sense of power, for I had put Nour out of countenance.

'*Weza*,' he said sullenly.

But Nour, as I should have known, was not one to submit to defeat. He shouted suddenly and my fingers pricked with fright.

'There, see the crocodile,' he yelled. 'See it move the water. See it smile.'

'There isn't a crocodile,' I said. 'They've all gone miles and miles upriver. The consul told me. There haven't been any here for years and years.'

'What does your consul know?' asked Nour, coming close to me. 'Your English consul with his English rivers and his little fish.'

I wanted to say, as I believed, that the consul was an English person of good sense with a proper grasp of facts, but I was too well brought up to state unequivocally that all foreigners, including Nour, were superstitious and given to exaggeration and unnecessary alarms.

'Do you want to see?' said Nour. 'See for yourself? Shall I show you?'

'Stop it,' I said.

Nour had taken me by the shoulders and was pushing me towards the pool. I slithered from his hands and sat down on the ground and he dragged me up. There was nothing for me to hold on to to prevent myself from getting closer and closer to the pool.

'There's bilharzia in that water,' I cried.

'Crocodiles,' said Nour, 'no bilharzia.' He pushed me as far as the trees and I seized a trailing branch.

'I'll tell your mother,' I said, and he let me go. I had been afraid.

I stumbled from the edge and backed away straight into Nour. His arms went round me and I shook.

'I'll tell your mother,' I said.

But this time he knew I didn't mean it.

*

Lili and Robert went away that week. They went to stay with friends in Scotland. Alone with my mother I had a sense of impropriety. It was no less incongruous for me to live with my mother than it was for Syl to live with his, or Nour with Marie Claire. Mothers should be left behind. I seemed fated to spend my time with them and it made me feel incomplete as though I were yet unborn. Such intimacy as life with my mother entailed should cease with parturition, and since Syl so resembled her in his attitude to me I could see no end to my continued childhood. Lili and Robert didn't oppress me. Childless, they were free, not constrained – constraining – links between birth and death. I wanted no children of my own, not because I disliked them, although I did – my step-sister and brother were the only small children I had experience of and they aroused no feelings in me but exasperation and distaste – but because I didn't want to be a mother with the weight of life and death on me. Perhaps the only creature to rouse what could be construed as a maternal sense in my heart had been the

101

Egyptian cat, and Nour had killed it.

*

I was once sitting in Syl's car when I heard Nour's voice.

I said aloud, 'No.'

'What?' said Mrs Monro from the back seat. We were going to a country pub for lunch. Just the three of us.

'Nothing,' I said. 'Sorry. I was thinking aloud.' I knew that Syl's mother, like my own, would consider talking to yourself the first sign of madness.

Nour hadn't killed the cat. He said he had and I believed him. After the first morning when it appeared in the garden I had gone on giving it food. It would eat anything – bread, even fruit – but I saved bits of meat for it when I could. We had a trysting-place, the cat and I, a strip of tiled pavement behind the villa surrounded by bushes for it to take refuge in should Marie Claire or Nour approach. Ahmed was dangerous too. He liked to please the family and if it wished ill to the starveling cat then so did he. He was a funny man and good at making people laugh. I laughed sometimes when he chased intruders from the garden, but I wished he hadn't been aware of the little cat, although I think he only wanted to frighten it away, not kill it.

Nour said (he really did say it) that I was disobedient to him to persist in feeding the cat. I had laughed at him more than I had laughed at Ahmed. I had been happy and thought he wouldn't mind. I had been wrong. Ahmed liked to be laughed at, but he was a peasant and Nour was, in his own estimation, a prince and I was of an English generation which would have felt free to laugh at the Grand Turk if it had been so inclined. It made Nour very angry. I had put on a show of contrition all day, and behind it had been incomprehension and fright. My pride of race didn't go as

102

deep as my fear of disapproval. I wouldn't have made a good martyr, for the frown of the tyrant alarmed me more than the threat of wild beasts or the rack. While knowing that being ingratiating was as unproductive as it was craven, I couldn't endure the wrath of those around me.

Marie Claire had some novels about English girls lost in the desert at the mercy of proud sheikhs, but those girls were as proud as the sheikhs themselves and defiant too – at least until near the end of the story – and the sheikhs were prepared to make some concessions themselves by that time. Nour would make none. He wore his mood wrapped tightly round like him like a *galabeah* until he was prepared to throw it off, and there was nothing I could do to change him.

'I choked the dirty thing,' said Nour, 'and threw it in the street for the dogs.'

But I was sure I had seen it after that, slinking, a shadow cat in the tree shadows, black as Egypt's night. No Englishman would have boasted mendaciously of killing a cat. Even Syl seemed fond of his mother's awful dog. It snuffled near the gear lever and he occasionally patted its head.

'It's nice here in the summer,' said Mrs Monro when we were sitting in the pub by a window overlooking the river and the distant fields.

An artificial log glowed in the manorial fireplace and I wondered whether she was admitting that it wasn't really very nice now, and how often Syl felt it as an obligation to take his mother for drives around the countryside. I saw the future with the three of us lunching regularly in this horrid pub at all the seasons of the year. Mrs Monro would say, 'It's nice here in the spring... or the autumn, or the winter...' And after the course of years perhaps I should respond, 'It was nice when the primroses were out...' or 'the leaves had turned golden...' or 'the snow was on the ground...' But by then I might have children and all I would be saying was 'Sit still', or 'Don't eat with your fingers', or 'Eat up all your peas.'

Mrs Monro had just admonished Syl, 'Don't eat with your fingers', because he had picked a roast potato straight from the vegetable dish and put it in his mouth. I waited for her to speak of peas, but she had no need. Syl was eating them all up without requiring any encouragement. She would be with us always, and I wouldn't have to say a word to her grandchildren because she would say them all. I thought of these imaginary children without hope and quite without fondness. Thinking of Jennifer and Christopher, I said 'No' aloud. It seemed to be becoming a habit.

'Yes,' said Syl, leaning towards me and smiling his smile. 'What do you think of her, Mum, talking to herself?'

'It's the first sign of madness,' said Mrs Monro.

I wished that I was less inhibited by my upbringing and could have done some extraordinary thing to confirm her diagnosis – danced on the table or stated that I wouldn't ally myself with a man with a face like a toothpaste advertisement. Or simply told the truth – told them there and now that it wasn't Syl's smile that repelled me but that I had an intuitive conviction that there was something unsound in him, something unwholesome by virtue of being undeveloped, something that would, sooner or later, cause me to turn on him with bitter cruelty as Nour had turned on me. It was probable, I thought, that what I disliked in him was what Nour had disliked in me, and that the whole world was mad. Why else should I still be yearning after a man whom I knew to be a murderer while shrinking from the innocent Syl whose only crime was that I found him unattractive? But I knew that reason was powerless to undo these matters and ate some Yorkshire pudding in silence.

'Look at those cows,' said Mrs Monro when the trifle had been put before us.

It was a boring remark, but at least she had thought of something to say. I could think of nothing, and Syl was busy with trifle, so I glanced, as bidden, out of the window. There was nothing unusual about the cows. They were only eating what remained of the summer's grass, but they had struck some chord in Mrs Monro.

'I was once chased by a herd of heifers,' she confided.

'Intrepid beasts,' said Syl through the jam and cream. He often teased his mother and I couldn't think why he bothered, for she seldom responded. Perhaps it was different when they were alone, and they laughed together.

'I had to jump over a hedge,' she said, 'and I tore my bloomers.'

I found this indelicate. I couldn't imagine her jumping over anything and I didn't think old ladies should mention their undergarments.

'Where was I?' asked Syl.

'It was long before you were born,' said his mother.

I knew I should show some interest in Mrs Monro's hedge-leaping girlhood. I even knew that if we talked about her past and all her life I might begin to like her, but I was thinking of a different countryside and different cattle and worrying about the oxen who ploughed the fields and turned the water wheels. The cows I could see grazed on and on, and I was trying to remember if I had ever seen an ox grazing instead of working. From the example of the cows before me it seemed that they were designed only and eternally to eat grass and, left to themselves, would never do anything else. I remembered the palms with clustered dates hanging like udders high in the air, and wished she had never mentioned the subject of cows.

'It was on the moors,' said Mrs Monro, laying down her

spoon with a decisive air. She hadn't quite finished her trifle, so Syl leaned over and scooped up what was left.

'There were three of us,' she continued, ignoring her son, 'but all the cows were chasing me. I wasn't wearing red and I could never think why they were chasing me and not the others.'

She looked puzzled for a moment, and I wondered if she really still worried about this ancient happening. Did the elderly have minds like old wardrobes stuffed to overflowing with useless memories and take them out sometimes and look at them and ask themselves why they were there? My own mind seemed full of memories already and I couldn't imagine storing away the new ones as years and years went by. Some surely must be discarded as outworn, but some wouldn't let themselves be forgotten. Some would take up for ever more space than they were entitled to – like my mother's wedding dress, shrouded in sheet linen, suspended in time, uncrushed by the other more workaday but less significant garments that crowded together as though they were cold, waiting in a queue, inmates of a *zenana* to be taken up or not at the Pasha's pleasure, promiscuously gathered, at the mercy of their owner. The nuns wore always the same habit. Even when they changed, the habit remained the same, blessed, sure and unobtrusive.

It was ironic that while most of the men I knew seemed inclined to some form of polygamy, Syl, now that he was getting older and had less energy, should have decided on a monogamous relationship with me. He had once assured me, earnestly unsmiling, that he would be faithful. I had said, in revulsion at the intimacy his words implied, that he could do what he liked, I didn't care; and he had taken this as evidence of a previously unsuspected sophistication in me. He had smiled then and said that despite my generosity he would give no cause for jealousy. Oh Syl.

How hopeless and ludicrous everything was: the seas of incomprehension, the misunderstandings that could never be cleared up because we seemed not only to speak different languages but to inhabit different countries. If I had told him I wished he was dead he would have seen this as a palimpsest of desire, but I only wished that he wasn't there.

I had wished Nour dead because he would not stay with me, and that had been a palimpsest of desire.

'I've been frightened of cows ever since,' said Mrs Monro, and I thought – her memories don't even have the moth.

*

When Lili came back from Scotland with a bottle of whisky and a biscuit box emblazoned with the tartan of the clan Campbell I told her that I was frightened of growing old.

'Well, it's that or die,' said Lili. 'You might as well hang around for as long as you can.'

I was disproportionately pleased to see her. She had the effect of an open window on a frowsty room, ice in a lukewarm drink, wind on a sullen sea. She was free of the shaming curbs of expedient morality. She would never smell of milk, or the urine of infants, or laundry-steam rising from linen indiscriminately washed. She wasn't a mother, and if she was a wife, she was, by conventional standards, a gloriously bad one.

'Did you have a good time?' my mother asked Robert as I whispered to Lili that I found old age unclean and a disgrace. When I was as old as Lili Syl would be an old, old man, but I didn't say that. I didn't want to think about it.

'You don't have to go along with it,' said Lili sitting down. I realised that I could have her full attention as long as I caught her interest, and I could only do this by telling the truth, for she could no more be bothered with the niceties of drawing-room small-talk than could a fox.

'You must wear false eyelashes,' she said, 'and very, very expensive scent, and you must never, never sit on a park bench with a person of your own age.'

'Is that all?' I asked. I liked this foolish image, which was so different from Mrs Monro.

'And you must try not to grow worse,' said Lili. 'Morality lapses as you get older and nothing seems to matter any longer.' She sounded serious and I knew that, this being so, she was talking about herself.

'I always wanted to die young and now it's too late,' she said. 'My mother died at the age I am myself and I never thought I'd be older than her. I was quite prepared to die – without giving it too much thought, you understand – and suddenly I find I've got up steam and I've puff-puffed past the station labelled "Death" and the track lies all before me, unsignposted.'

I saw myself chugging along a short track: a little side-shunting labelled 'Marriage' with unyielding buffers at the beginning and the end – cutting off the track and all the future. So I didn't say anything.

'The young are as good as gold. They fuss about fidelity. Even when they're not being it they're fussing about it. And they espouse causes and strike attitudes, and then after a while when they get old they think what-the-hell, and they start doing what they like and nothing matters at all. They still feel free to criticise the young though,' she added.

I always believed what she told me, but now as I considered her words I objected. 'I don't know any old people like that,' I said: 'not who are doing exactly what they like.' I was thinking of the mothers. But, so I found, was Lili.

'You have fallen into the common error,' she said. 'You

108

are taking it for granted that when I say "what they like" I mean sexual experience. Hmm?'

She looked at me unsmiling and I opened my mouth to protest that I was the last person in the world to take such a thing for granted, that I was the only person in the world who held a low opinion of sexual experience.

'You do not know,' said Lili, 'how many women would gladly put away for ever their suspender-belt and stockings – put them away with the relief of the weary warrior hanging up his shield after battle.'

I *had* assumed that everyone else was constantly in search of erotic adventure, of physical fulfilment, and I was affronted to discover that I was not, after all, unique. Realising that I was piqued by the recognition that I was not singular even in what I had considered an inadequacy, I convicted myself of lack of humility. Pride is the subtlest of sins, affording the most morally destitute some comfort, like a rat in the barren cell of the prisoner. I was pleased with this reflection, and so convoluted is the human mind that I ceased to take pride in my lack of pride and was proud that I had found myself capable of it. I was not perhaps as gutless as I had assumed.

'You are so young,' said Lili, as though youth were a shame and a disgrace. 'You have listened too much to men, to what the men say...'

She went on, but now I could hear another voice. Mother Joseph was saying '... and you see how the painter has painted her mouth so small. This is because Our Lady seldom spoke. She had no need for speech for she gave birth to – she uttered – The Word ...' and, standing before the icon, so perfect in its gilded stillness, I had thought of the bodies of men, land-locked and mute, and I had felt sorry for them.

'... and we all know what the weary warrior wants after

battle ...' Lili was saying. 'The trouble is it is unimaginable to him that his women don't want it in the same way.'

She was talking quite loudly now and Robert and my mother were both listening to her.

'Read a book by a man,' she said, adding severely, 'and I don't except *Madame Bovary* or *Anna Karenina* – and you will find that he has put breasts and a silken skirt and long-lashed eyes and lustrous hair on himself and filled his *poupée* with his own desires.'

I was sure that my mother neither understood nor agreed with what Lili was saying, but the mention of these classic works of literature compelled her to reveal at least her knowledge of their existence. She wasn't going to let her old classmate get away with showing off.

'I never really cared for *Madame Bovary*,' she said, 'but Tolstoy is another matter.'

Lili ignored her. 'No man,' she said, 'has ever portrayed a woman as she truly is.'

Robert spoke mildly. 'And no woman,' he said, 'has ever been able properly to portray a man.'

'I know that,' said Lili impatiently. 'Why should she bother?'

'There's never been a great woman composer,' said my mother with an air of triumph, not because she delighted in this deficiency of her sex, but because she thought it percipient to have noticed.

I wanted to say that women, since they uttered human beings, had no need to make a noise, that all the bluster of music was a sad cry because the world was unevenly divided, but I couldn't think of how to put it. I had always felt embarrassed and had to look at my feet in the presence of anyone playing any musical instrument, and had realised once when watching Syl spitting and squinting at his oboe that this was because it was irresistibly evocative of masturbation.

'People look silly playing a musical instrument,' I said.

'*You're* silly,' said my mother, getting angry because she wasn't used to converse of culture. She had had precisely the same expensive education as her friend and would never concede that she was not as clever.

'You talk tripe sometimes,' said Robert to his wife.

I wished that I could talk well, and could continue this conversation until animosity was dissipated and we could all stand on some common ground, but I knew enough to admit that this wouldn't happen, and that the longer the talk went on the further apart we should all grow.

Lili and I should talk alone. She showed no inclination to argue further, but lay back in her chair, smiling at Robert, and I saw that it was not, as I had believed, understanding and acceptance that her smile revealed, not that their marriage was so secure it could sustain itself in the face of any disagreement, but that Lili could afford to be pleasant because she had no scruples. I knew that tonight she would make love to another man. If Robert knew it too, as I thought he must, he seemed not to care. Perhaps it made for a safer relationship if, instead of arguing to a standstill, the party who felt herself misunderstood took her grievance elsewhere and satiated it in transgression. I was thinking, in contravention of everything I had been taught, that this casual immorality would be more wholesome than the hidden hatreds of marital strife. Everyone was amazed when my father left, but when I came to consider it I had been relieved. He had taken with him more badness than goodness, leaving not a vacuum, but a breathing space.

My mother seized the dangling reins of conversation. After all it was her house and the choice of topic should lie with her.

'I have my doubts about Cynthia,' she said. 'I don't trust her or her dressmaker to get the children's clothes right.'

She had posted off a length of pale blue silk for Jennifer's dress, and another of velvet in the same shade for Christopher's page-boy suit. She had enclosed patterns and detailed instructions, and while she hoped, for the sake of appearance at the wedding, that the children's clothes would be properly cut and fitted, she also hoped that between them Cynthia and her dressmaker would have made a pig's ear of the business.

'Let's go and see,' said Lili. 'We can drive down and have lunch in Winchester and be back by dinner time.'

My mother was startled at this suggestion. I had been there once or twice but she had never set foot in my father's new home.

'I don't know...' she said.

'I'm dying to see what Derek's landed himself with,' said Lili.

'You'll see them at the wedding,' said my mother.

'It's not the same,' said Lili. 'I want to see their little nest.'

'Well, I can suggest it to Cynthia,' said my mother. 'But I don't know what she'll say.'

We all knew it didn't matter what Cynthia said. If my mother decided to go, she would. And if she didn't, she wouldn't.

'Ring her now,' said Lili.

We listened to my mother talking to her successor, and I have never heard such an example of civilisation and restraint. Her resentment was buried deep. Lili was taken by a fit of mirth and lay with a cushion pressed to her nose. Above it her eyes glittered.

'I don't know why you're laughing,' said my mother coldly as she put down the phone.

'I'm not,' said Lili, sitting up and straightening her skirt.

'Yes, you are,' said my mother, and briefly she smiled too because in some ways she was no fool.

'We'll go on Thursday,' she added. 'And Cynthia says she'll give us a snack lunch.'

'Did she sound surprised?' asked Lili, and my mother said that, yes, she did rather. She smiled again.

'I don't have to come, do I?' I said.

'No, of course not,' said my mother, and now she sounded surprised. I understood that this was my mother's wedding, and although I was necessary to it I was expected to do nothing but be there and appear contented.

I, in my turn, was surprised to find how much I was looking forward to a day on my own, and mildly surprised at my mother's willingness to leave me to it.

'You can go and see Mrs M,' said my mother and I wondered whether her sense of grievance towards me was inclining her to spite.

*

When Thursday came and they had gone I found myself alone with Robert. I thought neither of us was thrilled, and Robert looked at his watch. Mrs Raffald looked at both of us, for she wanted to tidy the drawing-room and suspected that when all the coffee was drunk we would go in there. It was strange how difficult it was to be alone, especially as no one was anxious to be with me.

'All right?' said Robert from the door. 'I'll be back soon.'

'All right,' I said. Then I heard the door open again, and turned, thinking Mrs Raffald would be there with her things for tidying up, but it was Robert.

He said, 'Are you sure you don't want to come with me?'

I said blankly, 'No – I mean, yes – I mean, no thank you.'

'Sure?' he said.

'I've got a lot to do,' I said. 'I'll be all right.'

He looked worried – or perhaps he looked thwarted. It

did occur to me that since everyone seemed to be playing a game with rules unknown to me, Robert might not be concerned only that I would be bored by myself, but he might want me to go with him for reasons of his own. He was the same age as Syl, after all, and Syl wanted me to go with him for reasons of his own. There was a madness about and I couldn't tell whether it was within or without me, or either or neither. All the boundaries were blurred.

*

'What have you been doing?' asked my mother. She looked cheerful.

I had been to church, but I didn't tell her. I could imagine her discomfiture as a natural approval of this evidence of my religious feeling vied with her conviction that normal people did not go to church unless compelled by the Sabbath. I told her what she expected to hear – that I had not done anything much.

'Don't you want to know about the children's clothes?' she asked, adding that they had looked rather sweet.

'Except for the Peter Pan collars,' amended Lili. 'She'd put Peter Pan collars on them, so I took them off again, and fortunately there was enough stuff left to finish the neck lines.'

'If she'd stuck to the patterns,' said my mother, 'there'd have been no need, but Cynthia had to fiddle with them.' She still looked cheerful. 'Pork pies,' she said.

I could think of no response to this remark, so she went on to explain. 'Cynthia gave us pork pies and pickled cabbage.'

'How nasty,' I said tactfully. I loathed my father's new house, which seemed always to smell of damp washing, but her visit had clearly enlivened my mother. She would, I knew, have liked to categorise the shortcomings of her supplanter's domestic arrangements but was aware that it would seem too much like jealous triumph.

Happily for her, Lili had no such reservations and described the mess in the garden. I could visualise it. Mud and children's toys and a lopsided swing. Even the memory was depressing. The children of Egypt played in the dust-laden sunlight, and as far as I could tell they were happy.

Happiness was not the first quality to come to my mind when I thought of Jennifer and Christopher. They looked as though they knew already that life was no laughing matter. I should have felt sorry for them, but I didn't because I was really only sorry for myself and their problems weren't mine. They might have belonged to a different species. I wondered briefly whether my father had a tendency to marry women who would make their children unhappy, but it seemed an unfair reflection. I couldn't imagine myself making my children happy, having no conception of how to go about it. Oppression lay on me like a dead beast, not gaunt and stiff-legged like the animals which lay where they had dropped along the desert road, but soft and smothering like something from which the breath had only just gone. Once when I had thought Nour loved me I had delighted in a garden full of roses surrounding a villa where his aunts lived. The aunts had sat half-veiled in the evening, talking in Arabic and French and sometimes in English for me, but I hadn't listened. I had been remembering another rose garden lit by shafts of lightning and somebody telling me not to be afraid and to go to sleep. I hadn't been afraid. I had wanted to watch the roses lit by sudden light, but they wouldn't let me. The roses in the garden of the aunts were covered by a thin, barely perceptible layer of dust. Spoiled gardens, dusty flowers, small animals cowering under

115

wilting leaves. The convent garden harboured herbs and a yellow flowering vine flourishing over a falling wooden structure. I hadn't been aware of the dust in the convent garden. The nuns got rid of it. They were endlessly busy when they weren't praying and I remembered their surroundings as always faintly shining. They grew white lilies around a well and under the chapel wall for our Lady who had sojourned once in Egypt. I wondered why I hadn't had the wit to take the starveling cat to Mother Joseph as soon as I knew that Nour might kill it. It would have been safe there.

'You're very quiet,' said my mother.

I thought with sudden exasperation that of course I was quiet. I always had been. Marie Claire had once commended me on this negative virtue. 'You are no trouble,' she had said, lying back against the satin cushions, smelling of rosewater and musk. I don't know why it had occurred to her to make this observation. Perhaps Nour had burdened her with noisy, tearing girls who had shattered the afternoon calm with screams of merriment and wild gestures, or frenzied weeping. I moved so quietly I barely stirred the dust, yet now in the English winter I could hear a spectral echo of angry laughter and I thought it was my own.

Marie Claire had written to say she couldn't come to the wedding and had sent a present of yet more tablecloths and napkins. 'How useful,' my mother had remarked. I hadn't read the letter. I imagined Marie Claire coming to England in the cold to be present at my marriage. She would have worn her furs and her jewellery and she would have struck an even odder note than Lili. She might have made Nour come with her, because she refused to travel alone. They both looked exotic even standing by the Nile and would have seemed remarkably out of place among us. It was perfectly possible that they could have come, and yet unthinkable. My imagination failed.

'I feel a bit deranged,' said Lili. 'I think it must be something to do with the pickled cabbage. Or perhaps it's just the effect of the Peter Pan collars. Cynthia is a remarkably inefficient woman.'

My mother looked pleased. 'I know what you mean,' she said.

'There's no need for such messiness,' said Lili. 'Messiness makes me feel like hitting someone. I get this inclination to take a broom and a pail and tidy up. I would start by throwing Cynthia away and I would sit the little children on a shelf while I swept the crumbs off the floor.'

'The place wasn't actually dirty,' said my mother with conspicuous justice, 'but it is dreadfully untidy. She doesn't seem to put anything away. There are clothes everywhere.'

'And such clothes,' cried Lili, who seemed intent on gratifying my mother. 'She dresses like the offspring of the vicar and his cleaning lady. When she goes to parties she will wear not a party frock but a summer frock with a bow at the neck and a tie round the waist. She will undoubtedly wear a summer frock for the wedding.'

'She's quite kind,' I said.

Lili went towards the drinks table. 'Where stands the sun in relation to the yard-arm?' she enquired rhetorically, pouring a Gin and It. 'As if it mattered. I drank brandy for breakfast in Tanta.'

'I'll have a martini,' said my mother. She was sitting back relaxedly and looking more contented than she had for some time. 'Margaret?'

'Yes please,' I said, all at once looking forward to the mild dulling of the senses, the ease which the evening drinks induced.

'It is better not to drink in the daytime,' said Lili. 'Not so much because of the liver but because it spoils the effect of the first drink of the evening.' She was wearing a burgundy-coloured dress of fine corduroy and reminded me herself of foreign wine.

'I know,' I said.

'You shouldn't need it,' said my mother remembering her responsibilities, 'not at your age.'

'I have had this dress for ten years,' remarked Lili. 'I was ten years younger when I had it made. You see this tiny patch where the material is paler. That is where I spilled vodka on it the day I wore it for the first time.'

My mother gazed at her enquiringly with a so-what expression on her face.

'I have been drinking all my life,' explained Lili. 'And I am growing older. But my clothes are not. My clothes remain the same. They never wear out because I look after them so well and they stay young while I ... I ...'

'Portrait of Dorian Grey,' interrupted my mother triumphantly.

'Quite,' said Lili.

'Don't they date?' asked my mother. 'I find I have to change my wardrobe every other year or so.'

'Not really,' said Lili.

'What about hem-length?' enquired my mother.

It would be impossible to accuse Lili of being ill-dressed, but if she wore the same clothes for decade after decade while my mother did not, then there was something wrong somewhere and my mother was suspecting that, implicit in the situation, lay criticism of her taste and judgement.

'I always keep the same hem-length,' said Lili. 'Mid-calf.' She spoke casually without looking at my mother, and changed the subject. 'Did Marie Claire say why she couldn't come?'

'Oh, some family business,' said my mother. 'They have

those dozens of cousins and aunts and there's always some sort of crisis going on.'

As far as I could gather, Nour's father had taken on responsibility for all his sisters, married or not, and for their offspring, and since his death Marie Claire had assumed the burden. Eventually it doubtless would fall to Nour. I wondered what sort of job he would make of it. I had once imagined that I too might one day be involved in that large, confusing family with its extended degrees of affinity. I wondered how it could be that I was going to marry Syl.

'I don't want to marry Syl,' I said, surprised to hear that I had spoken aloud.

'Don't be silly,' said my mother.

'Have another martini,' said Lili.

'I *don't*,' I said.

'Now look here ...' began my mother.

'I want to be a nun,' I said. I had wanted to be a nun before Nour had made me love him with his golden hair and his golden face and his golden eyes. I wondered how long it would be before I stopped loving him. I had loved God before Nour. I had been a vessel of pure water and I had been spilled. I had loved God more than I had loved Nour and I had betrayed him. I had rendered myself purposeless.

'You can't change your mind at this point,' said my mother, carefully reasonable, and ignoring this imbecile talk of nuns.

Lili looked thoughtful, but I didn't know what she was thinking about. I was angry with her for not saying anything, not doing anything. I still had a formless feeling that she understood me where my mother did not. Perhaps it was despair that made me believe there was one person in the world who might know that I was in despair.

'Do have another martini,' said my mother. 'Lili, you have one too.'

119

'Shall we all get very drunk?' suggested Lili.

'There's no need for that,' said my mother. 'Margaret is merely suffering from pre-wedding nerves. She should have an early night.'

'Why don't we take her out to dinner?' said Lili. 'I'll drive us to Soho.'

'We've just got back from Southampton,' said my mother, as though this circumstance presented a total barrier to further movement. 'What about Robert?'

'Robert will be all right,' said Lili. 'I think we should definitely go out.'

'Why?' asked my mother.

'It would be enjoyable,' said Lili. 'It would be interesting to try a new restaurant. It would remind us of the days of our youth mixing with Greeks and Arabs and Armenians in strange corners of the world.'

I still couldn't imagine my mother mixing with foreigners anywhere.

'We could go to Rules,' she said doubtfully, 'but we haven't booked.'

'Let's go somewhere more *farouche*,' said Lili coaxingly. 'Somewhere we won't see anyone we know.'

Maybe my mother thought it would take my mind off the convent, for she agreed.

Lili could be charmingly manipulative, but I would have thought my mother proof against her. I had no desire to go out, but it would be one way of getting through the evening.

Sitting in the back of the car I watched the suburbs going by under the street lights. They hadn't the appeal of the stinking lanes fitfully lit by naphtha flares in the *souks* when a fair went on long into the night.

*

120

Lili sang as she drove.

The restaurant was in a back street and was small and half-empty. My mother looked round with an expression of misgiving. 'Why here?' she enquired, too loudly.

'I was told about it,' said Lili. 'They do delicious *moules marinières* and they're not mean with the garlic.'

'Well, I don't know,' said my mother, extremely dubiously, but she permitted herself to be led to a table and sat down.

'I hope it's clean,' she said. 'It doesn't look terribly clean. I hope there aren't any cockroaches. Cynthia's house this morning – and now this.'

'Not your day is it, darling,' said Lili consolingly. 'Just wait till you try the *moules*.'

'I'm not sure I want *moules*,' said my mother. 'I'm never sure about shellfish.'

'They get them fresh every day,' said Lili.

'How do you know?' asked my mother.

'I was told,' said Lili, 'by the person who told me about this place.' She looked round. 'It has a certain character, you must admit.'

'When people say that about restaurants,' said my mother grimly, 'it usually means cockroaches.'

I thought this rather witty of my mother. Lili seemed able to make both her and Syl's mother passingly amusing.

I was sitting with my back to the door. I felt a draught as it opened, and half turned. Nobody came in, but as I looked round I saw my mother staring past me, her mouth open.

'Wasn't that ...?' she said. 'Did I see ...?'

'Who?' asked Lili casually, lighting a cigarette and shading the lighter flame with her hand.

'I could have sworn that was Syl,' said my mother. 'He looked straight at me and went straight out again.'

'He works somewhere round here,' said Lili. 'Perhaps it

121

was him.'

'At this time?' said my mother. 'And why did he go like that?'

'Perhaps he had a secret assignation,' said Lili. She looked up, into my eyes, and grinned.

My mother recovered herself. 'Don't be ridiculous,' she said, 'I must have been mistaken. The light's none too good in here.'

The *moules marinières*, by the way, were unexceptional.

*

'And this is my present to the bride,' said Syl. He had been very noticeably kind over the past few days: thoughtful, and seeming more mature and sensible, as though the imminence of marriage had indeed begun to bring about that change of which my elders spoke – the settling down, as it was called. There had been no unexplained nights away and no displays of petulance, and when he set off through the gates of his house he drove slowly and with care. Nobody had spoken of this new responsible attitude, because to do so would be to admit that his behaviour had previously left something to be desired, and my mother had spent too much time in implicit denial of this to waste it all now. I wasn't deceived, for Nour had been kind when I had been what he called 'good', and I had thought that a new Nour had been born who was made for me, designed for all my needs and desires, and we would be unchangingly happy together until the end of time. I had thought that for about five days.

'Oh Syl,' my mother said effusively as he laid the oblong package on the drawing-room table. 'What is it?'

Clearly it was I who should have spoken these words, but already I had a feeling that I knew what the brown paper

122

and the ribbed cardboard concealed, and I wasn't going to say a word until time or circumstance compelled me.

'Open it, Margaret,' cried my mother, and as I made no move she herself ripped off its coverings.

'Oh, how lovely,' she said less effusively, for after all it was only one of Robert's paintings.

*

I knew as I was doing it that I shouldn't be following them, through the snake-laced paths to the river in the moonlight, to the broken house with the pigeon tower: that shame would be the result – my shame, for I cared nothing what their feelings might be. I was used to shame. I had felt it for my mother before my father left when she would intercept his post, putting certain violet-scented envelopes into the pocket of her dress and steaming them open in the kitchen after he had left for work. The indignity of peering into other people's intimacies had appalled me, quite over-powering the acquired, accepted knowledge that reading other people's letters was one of the things that wasn't done. I had felt all my life that lavatory and bedroom doors should be kept firmly shut, for fear of what they might reveal. My mother had taught me that, just as she had taught me to change my underclothes daily and not blow my nose in public. Walking silently and in stealth over the harsh grass I remembered all the things an English gentlewoman shouldn't do, and the thing my mother had done.

Then when I came near the broken house and stood in the moon shadow I could hear and see nothing. I don't know how long I stood there while the world turned. After a while I saw Nour standing on the low wall gleaming naked in the dark light, looking defenceless and young. He knew I was there, for he called softly, 'Margaret, Margaret', and I went towards him.

The fortune-teller lay on her back behind the low wall and she was dying, or perhaps she was dead, for her eyes were open and she looked up at the stars. Her clothes were wet with blood.

Nour said, 'You must help me now, Margaret.' He added, 'The jackals will come tonight and lick up the blood.'

He sounded hopeful. I wondered why the girl was clothed and Nour naked, but I asked no questions.

'I have here part of an old plough,' said Nour.

He now sounded as though he were beginning a lecture and I thought he must have learned that intonation from his tutors. I expected him to continue, but he knelt and pushed the rusty metal through the brightly coloured rope that bound the fortune-teller's waist. Then between us we carried her to the river and rolled her in and Nour washed himself at the edge of the crocodile pool. I don't think I had any blood on my hands, for I had held her ankles just below the silver bracelets.

'Where did you get the knife?' I asked. Nour was holding it now above his head.

'It was hers,' he said and hurled it into the pool.

I watched it go regretfully because it was a beautiful Berber knife. I wondered why Nour had killed her and decided she had probably laughed at him.

He put on his shirt and shorts and took my hand. We went back to the villa hand in hand and no one ever knew we had been out, or if they did they didn't say.

Alone in bed I wondered for the first time whether the girl had been truly dead when we threw her into the river. Sometimes I still wonder.

*

124

'Well?' said my mother impatiently.

'I know this one was your favourite,' said Syl. 'We'll hang it in the bedroom where you can see it when you wake up.'

I gazed at the picture of the crocodile pool and all I could think of to say was, did the gallery owner give you a discount because you're a friend of Robert's? But I didn't, of course. Syl's mad little meannesses were not to be mentioned.

*

In the end my mother had invited fewer than fifty people. The wedding was not going to be the one she had dreamed of. She must have realised some years before that I wasn't headed in the direction of St Margaret's, Westminster, but she had still intended the occasion to glitter, a bright milestone in our uneventful lives. I knew how she envisaged it – all sparkle: the glass, the cutlery, the champagne, the eyes of the bride; gleaming white napery, carnations and maidenhair fern swaddled at the stem in silver paper; fallen flakes of expensive pastry, and the smart aroma of smoked salmon and asparagus blending subtly with the scent of flowers and wine; loud voices and muted laughter; sometimes a discreet tinkle of broken glass, because at a good wedding some breakage was unavoidable, indeed desirable, and evidence of an expansive generosity. The weddings I had been to had been like that, quite different from the wedding parties in the villages along the Nile: a deafening noise of drums and flutes, bright hot colours and people saying words I couldn't understand. My mother's hat, I thought, would have looked very out of place at one of those Nilotic feasts. Despite the time of year she intended to dress herself in mauve silk, a coat and skirt faced with regal purple and embellished with a cream lace *jabot*. Her hat was mauve plush with a veil. Lili had given the outfit her qualified approval. 'Cut the *jabot*,' she had advised. 'Wear a string of pearls if you must, but cut the *jabot*.'

'I need the *jabot*,' my mother said, 'to hide the crêpiness of the throat.'

'Once you start thinking like that,' said Lili, 'you might as well go round dressed up like Whistler's mother.'

Lili was going to wear a crimson redingote of stiff taffeta with dull pewter buttons all down the front, a skull cap of crimson velvet atop her rusty curls, grey gun-metal stockings and gloves, and Egyptian crimson slippers. She looked a little peculiar, but she would make everyone else look pitifully ordinary.

'Don't you think your grey ...' my mother would say to her, 'or perhaps that nice beige facecloth coat-dress ...' But Lili said there were few enough times when she got the chance really to dress up and she was going to now.

The caterers had been in and out with boxes and covered trays. They were polite, professional and subservient, and reminded me irresistibly of undertakers.

*

My father arrived with his wife and children two days before the wedding. They had come only from Southampton where his shipping firm had now placed him, but Cynthia and the children couldn't be expected to face the rigours of the festivities on the same day that they had driven seventy-odd miles. Cynthia preferred to endure a night under the roof of the woman she had superseded. I thought this unexpectedly brave of her until I realised that she had no sense of incongruity whatsoever and wasn't aware that her presence might be unwelcome. She treated my mother as an older woman, not so much by deferring to her as by assuming that they had nothing at all in common, and never could have had. In one way this eased the situation, since it occluded any sense of unseemly rivalry, but it annoyed my mother.

Everything about Cynthia annoyed my mother, including the confusion attending her arrival. We stood in the doorway watching as she backed out of the car, immediately reaching into the back seat to extract her children. With them came carrier bags, dolls, bears, sandwiches, apple cores, orange peel and biscuit packets. A roll of lavatory paper fell on the drive and unravelled. My mother sighed. Then my father opened the boot. He had not so far looked at us waiting, a welcome party, in the doorway. Cynthia dropped a bag, out of which fell a beach ball and a clockwork mouse. My mother rolled her eyes but we stepped forward to help.

'Well, here we all are,' observed my father, forced into recognition of our presence.

Lili kissed him first, elaborately on both cheeks. Then she kissed Cynthia in the same fashion. Cynthia was surprised by this and dropped another bag. Then Lili kissed the children, who appeared less startled than alarmed. One of them stumbled over the beach ball and set it moving, and some of us ran after it. My father kissed my cheek in passing and asked how his little girl was.

'Fine,' I said.

'I've put you in the Blue room,' my mother told Cynthia, 'and the children in the dressing-room next door to it.'

None of our rooms was usually referred to in this stately manner, but my mother was determined to wring some enjoyment out of the situation. It was a little too early however to start frightening Cynthia, for she was engrossed with getting what seemed to be all her household effects upstairs.

127

'Bring Christopher's you-know-what,' she instructed my father, and my mother gave the object in question a meaningful glance. I gathered that in her opinion Christopher was now far too old to need a portable pot. Unfortunately Cynthia intercepted the look and explained. 'He won't do jobbies without it,' she said worriedly, going upstairs empty-handed while my father followed with the luggage.

'Aaugh,' observed Lili, lighting a cigarette, 'what a *revolting* thing to say.'

My mother looked gratified.

'I suspected she was unbalanced,' said Lili, 'when I saw that she had ashtrays fixed to leather straps on the arms of her chairs.'

'And no linen hand-towels in the bathroom,' said my mother with satisfaction.

Poor Cynthia, I thought, but my sympathy was wasted. Cynthia was oblivious of everything but herself and the children. This being the case I foresaw that she would inevitably go on putting her foot in it. The pre-occupied frequently do, since their minds are not on the manners and mores of polite society and they express their anxieties without thought of the likely consequences. I was different, having no pre-occupations apart from self-consciousness. This did not prevent me from making gaffes, but mine were in a different category – errors not merely of taste but of spirit – and in the main mine were sins of omission. I knew that it was inadvisable to attempt to paddle in deep waters. I tried always to stand quite still in the illusory shallows.

*

It hadn't occurred to me to scream at the sight of the dead fortune-teller or even to step back aghast, my hand to my heart, as the girls in the books would have done. Murder was

128

a solecism and it would have been ill-bred to draw attention to it. A gentlewoman shouldn't make scenes, any more than she should read other people's letters. It was incorrect to appear to mind too much about anything. I adhered to this code more rigorously than my mother did, for often the pupil takes the teachings more seriously than does the tutor.

Besides I didn't care that Nour was a murderer. I didn't care that the girl was dead, except that it seemed unnatural that she should be. I had a long time ago, somewhere, seen a dead kingfisher, and that had been incongruous too and disquieting.

Once Nour said that he had found her dead, once that she had killed herself. And once he wondered aloud whether Ahmed had killed her because she had trespassed in the garden. He was trying to regain his innocence. I could have told him it was impossible. I found his state no more regrettable than my own. Perhaps I was a moral idiot, or perhaps I was right and sin once committed has fewer degrees than we believe.

All I really cared about was that he didn't love me. If ever he might have done – and I knew in those moments when I could bear to be honest that he never would have – he couldn't now. No one can love a person who knows a secret about him that he would prefer not to know himself. Narcissus does not sit by his pool to see ruined and rusted detritus and the floating, bloated bodies of dead toads. And Nour could never be sure that I saw him as guiltless as he saw himself. The prince had blundered, to put it no higher. I had betrayed God for a blundering prince.

*

It was some days since I had been to the summer-house.

'Darling,' said my mother, relaxed now that the wedding was so close and I hadn't yet disgraced her completely, 'go and see if the cactus is flowering. It will be so lovely if it comes out for the wedding.'

It was quite early in the morning or I should have suspected my mother of drinking. I stared at her.

'Well?' she said, turning from where she was making breadcrumbs at the kitchen table.

'Why?' I asked, and I sounded half-witted. I couldn't see that it would make the slightest difference to the occasion whether the cactus flowered or not. My mother seldom called me 'darling', and while I thought her fondness for her cactuses slightly silly I hadn't imagined her to be as sentimental as she was suddenly proving. Perhaps because I was so soon to be out of her care she was already growing careless, feeling free to express emotions that might previously have seemed like indulgence, might have spoiled me. She had a great detestation of a spoiled child.

She flushed when she saw my face, but it was with annoyance.

'It means good luck,' she said. 'There should always be something flowering, even for a winter wedding.'

I thought Lili was amazing. She had sown seeds of superstition in my mother and made them grow. It was a feat far more remarkable than my mother's cultivation of her cactus. I was sure that it had been Lili who had given my mother this idea. My mother's only previous obeisances to fortune had been touching wood and throwing spilled salt over her left shoulder to blind the devil. There was something crafted about this flowering myth, something touchingly, repellently obvious – like the gift which the honey-curled innocent is deputed to hand to the rich and evil-tempered old relation. What, I asked myself, was Lili up to? I felt that now I had been betrayed. It seemed as though she had been trying to help my mother sweeten the occasion – garland it with pretty conceits, as people pile wreaths on corruption.

'Who said so?' I asked without subtlety.

'Nobody said so,' squawked my mother. 'I don't *believe* it, but it's a pretty thought. *Isn't* it?' she added angrily as I still stood gazing at her.

'Yes,' I said.

'I'll go down myself later,' said my mother, 'but I'm busy with the stuffing for the duck. Go and get some fresh air.'

The air was more than fresh. It was freezing in the garden. It was nearly as cold in the summer-house. There was a bud on the cactus but it looked unpromising. There was a small bottled gas-heater in the corner and I wondered if my mother had instructed the jobbing gardener to warm the place up further to encourage the thing to flower. There was a pile of my books where I had left them half-read. And there were some torn scraps of red crêpe paper on the floor. The moorish arches of the summer-house windows framed a vista of dead grass and deciduous trees beyond the broken hedge of evergreens through which Syl entered my mother's garden when he came to call. Some black birds flew by with a stunned weariness like the survivors of a disaster. Winter must seem like a disaster to birds, and rain was on its way. I didn't care. I picked up a bit of red paper and twisted it in my fingers. It was the colour of the doubtless poisonous berries which gleamed here and there in the hedge and it stained my hands. The summer-house was always untidy because my mother stored things in it besides using it as a haven for her cactus. Garden chairs and umbrellas were stacked in a corner with some flower pots. The cushions along the ledge smelled damp, and when I sat on them they felt chilly even through my tweed skirt. The paraffin heater which was left on constantly may have been sufficient to support life in the cactus, but it wasn't enough to comfort me. I sat under a travelling rug and looked at my fingernails.

Lili tapped on the window before she came in, wearing a scarlet wool coat with a huge collar. I hadn't seen it before. The collar stood up round her head and her rusty curls rested on it.

'You look warm,' I said from under my rug.

'I'm not really,' said Lili. 'I'm beginning to pine for the banks of the Nile.'

'Do you think that thing is going to flower?' I asked.

'Mmm,' said Lili.

*

I sat holding myself still against the cold. I wished Lili had stayed with me, hung about with cigarette smoke and laughing. I could still smell cigarettes. There were butts lying on the wooden floor. I missed Lili in her scarlet cloak and her stench of scent and cigarettes. Nour had smoked incessantly and so had some of his aunts. My mother and Syl disapproved of the habit. My father didn't smoke. Nor did Cynthia. The house was smoke-free when Lili went out. At the moment it smelled of food and wedding preparations and children. Cynthia had said they couldn't go out because they might catch cold. My mother was trapped in her own house with her ex-husband and his new family. Nobody was laughing and the children were grizzling. I wondered if they would be happier on the banks of the Nile playing in the dust with the brown babies and the children or leaning against the knees of the covered, cigarette-smoking aunts. I pictured Syl's cold house invaded by crying children and wondered if I could alter the atmosphere sufficiently to make it bearable by taking to

132

cigarettes. It seemed like a counsel of despair. I imagined myself creeping about in the night dropping smouldering stubbs in conveniently inflammable corners till all the house burned down. Perhaps if I smoked in bed Syl would sleep in the spare room. Perhaps I could drop ash on the things I cooked and he would refuse to eat them and starve to death. I wondered if it was fair to wish somebody dead because he was going to marry me. I wondered if I was truly eternally wicked and how many people had turned to destruction because they had no strength in them. I wondered if the venom of weakness was more dangerous than the rage of power, more insidious with its content of despair, and if when the world failed it would be because it was heavy with inertia and the tears of deceit, not the fires of wrath. I wondered what would happen if I laughed at Syl. He might kill me.

I stayed in the summer-house while it rained. The rain of winter was like the tears of the old: not sorrowful and not kind, bitter. Self-pity was a wearisome emotion. I wished I was dead, but I had been too well brought up to snatch at death without being invited. It was not there for the asking but had to be deserved or – sometimes – offered as a gift. I thought it remarkable how few people appreciated this offer. Did they like the rain and the pain and the boredom which constituted life? Perhaps the death-fearers perceived life differently from me. For me it was being a vessel of evil afloat in a sea of evil. If I broke, it would take the power of God to separate my elements from the elements of the sea – and why, I asked myself, should he bother, since if I took my own life it would be in full knowledge of what the act entailed? I drifted on a sluggish tide of badness unable to see help or hope, and silent: blind as a worm, as a bottle, faceless and limbless, incapable of any cry or gesture or expression that might call the rescuer to me. I reminded myself that she who has scuttled the ship cannot in all conscience summon the lifeboat, even were she able. I waited.

Lili had gone to the gallery, for Robert's exhibition was over and there were things she had to discuss with the owner. My mother had said earlier that Lili must remind him not to forget the wedding. 'What?' I had asked, thinking it impossible that she would have invited a virtual stranger – of whom she had been determined to disapprove – to my wedding. She had ignored me and I hadn't repeated my question.

'I think you should see Syl,' said my mother. 'He'll cheer you up. Perhaps he'll take you out to dinner or for a drive.'

Oh God. I said, 'Mother, I am truly all right. I don't want to go out to dinner or for a drive. I don't want to see Syl.' *I don't want to see Syl.*

'Rubbish,' said my mother, going to the telephone.

'Hallo?' she said. 'Ah, Mrs Monro.'

Serve you right, I thought. Now you'll have to talk about the weather and she may go on to complain about the government.

But the conversation was very brief.

'Oh,' said my mother. 'Oh, all right. Thanks.'

She put the telephone down slowly and I could see her wondering what to tell me.

'Has he gone out?' I asked.

'Er, yes,' said my mother. She paused. 'He had to see a client.'

'I didn't know solicitors saw clients in the evening,' I said. I was beginning to cultivate an air of *faux naiveté* to disguise my real ignorance of the world and I wouldn't have blamed my mother if she'd thrown the decanter at me.

'Well, they do,' she said shortly. She said no more but left the room by gradual degrees, humming a little,

134

straightening a cushion, pushing a silver snuff-box nearer to the centre of the table, until she reached the door and went out to the kitchen.

I wondered what I would have done if I had discovered Syl, redhanded, standing over a dying girl behind the summer-house. It occurred to me that trysting places – summer-houses and ruined pigeon towers, hidden strips of tiled pavement – are by their very nature secret, and therefore perilous. Love and death happen in the unfrequented ways. A laugh at the wrong moment and a poor body, hoped-for vehicle of pleasure, would lie, wide-eyed, transfixed by steel with no one to know. My confessor had said I should have told the authorities, but he didn't know Egypt. I knew that the authorities would not have pursued the son of the Pasha, and anyway the girl was gone without trace to the bottom of the crocodile pool. I hoped that Allah had washed away the fingerprints of the murderer, not for his sake, but for hers. It was hard to be born formed and distorted by the mother body, intolerable to enter eternity fumbled and bruised by the hands of a stranger.

I would have screamed if I had apprehended Syl the murderer because I cared nothing for his good opinion. I would have run, screaming, to the real house where the lights were on. I would have screamed 'Mother' and 'Police'. I would have been glad. I would have been free.

*

I remember little about the night before the wedding. The house was full of people. Syl and his mother came for martinis and she brought her little dog to show to Jennifer and Christopher. The dog didn't like the children, nor the children the dog. That part was a failure. The gallery

135

owner was there and, it seemed, was staying overnight. I found this most strange and asked Lili why it was so. She looked at me oddly.

'Weren't you listening?' she asked.

'No,' I said.

'Your mother invited him after the opening night,' she explained. 'They got on so well and had so much in common.'

'Oh,' I said. After a while it became clearer to me. My mother was unwontedly attentive to the gallery owner, especially when Cynthia was in the vicinity. My mother didn't care to appear as a woman without a man on this occasion, loaded as it was with hints of lubricity. Lili had a man, Cynthia had my mother's erstwhile man, I was about to have a man, and my mother had refused to be allied with Mrs Monro as a spare and unwanted female. This realisation made me think less of her.

My father, when he could be, was unwontedly attentive to me. Cynthia dogged him but he did his best to talk to me. Unfortunately he could think of little to say and silences kept falling between us. In the end I was quite relieved that Cynthia was there. Her conversation was unmemorable but it made the awkwardness less obvious.

Syl and his mother left early. My father, still trying to make things go with a swing, said, 'Yes, you'd better have an early night tonight, old man. Ho, ho.'

I knew this was the sort of remark that was made at weddings, but my awareness made me feel no less ill.

Lili handed me a drink. She plied me with whisky until the horrible evening became as blurred as the boundaries of madness, and I remember nothing more.

*

136

I also remember little of the following morning until the moment we set off for the summer-house. My mother went to early Mass because it was *comme il faut* but didn't even ask me to accompany her. She had looked at my face, haggard with hangover, and left.

She brought the parish priest back for breakfast and we crowded into the morning-room because the dining-room was being readied for the more important wedding breakfast which loomed in the afternoon. I hadn't bothered to dress, since there seemed no point when I should soon have to don the garment which hung over a chair in my bedroom. I sat in my nightdress and dressing-gown and drank tea.

Lili was already in her redingote and refused to sit down for fear of creasing it. She had her hat on too and looked alert and excited. I was drearily disappointed in her. She left the room and I supposed she had gone to charm the caterers who were adorning the table with maidenhair fern.

After a while she came back smelling of cold air and cigarette smoke.

'It's out,' she said.

'What's out?' asked my mother, who had a great deal on her mind.

'The cactus, darling,' said Lili.

'It *can't* be,' said my mother, now also looking elaborately excited. 'It showed no signs yesterday.'

'Well, it's out now,' said Lili.

'I must go and see,' cried my mother, vivacious for the sake of the gallery owner.

'No,' said Lili. 'Wait until everyone's finished their breakfast and you can all go and see.'

This idea appealed to my mother. 'We can go and toast it,' she said, 'with champagne.'

'What?' asked Cynthia. She had somehow managed to

137

cram both her children on her lap. They were crying a
little.

My mother took on a more staid expression and adjusted
her voice to instruct. 'My winter-flowering cactus,' she said.
'It's a sign of great good fortune if it flowers on the wedding
day.' This slight exaggeration of the myth I felt sure Lili
had constructed gave her pleasure and she smiled at the
gallery owner.

'You *must* come too,' said Lili to me. 'Go and put on
something warm.'

*

An hour later we all set off down the lawn carrying glasses
and a couple of bottles.

'Where's Lili?' asked Robert as we reached the
summer-house.

Lili was already there, and so was Syl.

She still wore her hat and her redingote although it was
utterly unbuttoned and she had clearly ceased to care
whether it was creased or not, but Syl was naked except for
his socks and shirt. I thought, with the first touch of pity I
had ever felt for him, that he must be rather cold.

*

This is my last memory of Lili and another one I shall keep
until the day I die. We had all witnessed the scene; those
who hadn't crowded to the door peered through the
moorish windows to see the winter-flowering cactus and I
noticed that it was made of crêpe paper. She was
always clever with her hands. The gallery owner
shouted, in an outraged roar, 'Lili.' And I thought –
Lili has slept with every man present with the possible

138

exception of Father O'Flynn. And then I thought that what would have upset my mother most was that Mrs Raffald who was helping with the preparations had also come to see the cactus flower.

*

I went back to bed, and I never knew how the caterers were dismissed and the wedding guests turned away, the cake and the maidenhair fern disposed of and the parish priest returned to his church.

*

The day came when I was aware that I had been forgiven, that I was free of Hell. I think perhaps that such things happen in eternity and not in time and that we, mortal and profane, can only gradually realise the movements of God: that he is generous and unassuming in these matters, not demanding scenes of reconciliation, merely our souls' health. I was filled with a sense of flowering, of abundance and gratitude, which related me for a while to infinity. The feeling lessened, of course, for only the saints can bear to live close to God, but sometimes now when I listen to the convent bells ringing with the cry from the minaret, and I look at the lilies under the convent wall where we plant them in memory of Our Lady who sojourned for a while in Egypt, I feel another sense of gratitude. To Lili. For surely to make a great fool and spectacle of yourself for the sake of another is a form of martyrdom.

The fact that she also enjoyed it seems immaterial. I had caught a glimpse of her face and remembered that she had been a dancer and had capered on the stage to the gaze of strangers. She had hated it too. She had given up a lot for my sake – dignity, and the goodwill of my mother, although I don't suppose that bothered her too greatly. Robert would forgive her. He always had. It was a strange martydom. She had offered not so much a sacrifice as a gift. What she had given was of value only to me, and she had not in reality harmed or impoverished herself beyond redemption. I have long since ceased attempting to follow the processes by which God works out his purpose, but I know he sent me Lili. For who but he – or she – would have conceived of a wedding present so original as the scene in the summer-house?

I remembered one day what she had been saying all those years ago, seated on the hummock of harsh grass. She had been speaking of love and I hadn't understood her, and she had waved her cigarette, and Robert had asked her if she would rather live for the rest of her life without smoking or without love, and she had replied, 'What do you think?'

My only regret is that no one answered her, and now I shall never know.

FOR THE BEST IN PAPERBACKS, LOOK FOR THE 🐧

In every corner of the world, on every subject under the sun, Penguin represents quality and variety – the very best in publishing today.

For complete information about books available from Penguin – including Pelicans, Puffins, Peregrines and Penguin Classics – and how to order them, write to us at the appropriate address below. Please note that for copyright reasons the selection of books varies from country to country.

In the United Kingdom: Please write to *Dept E.P., Penguin Books Ltd, Harmondsworth, Middlesex, UB7 0DA*

In the United States: Please write to *Dept BA, Penguin, 299 Murray Hill Parkway, East Rutherford, New Jersey 07073*

In Canada: Please write to *Penguin Books Canada Ltd, 2801 John Street, Markham, Ontario L3R 1B4*

In Australia: Please write to the *Marketing Department, Penguin Books Australia Ltd, P.O. Box 257, Ringwood, Victoria 3134*

In New Zealand: Please write to the *Marketing Department, Penguin Books (NZ) Ltd, Private Bag, Takapuna, Auckland 9*

In India: Please write to *Penguin Overseas Ltd, 706 Eros Apartments, 56 Nehru Place, New Delhi, 110019*

In Holland: Please write to *Penguin Books Nederland B.V., Postbus 195, NL–1380AD Weesp, Netherlands*

In Germany: Please write to *Penguin Books Ltd, Friedrichstrasse 10–12, D–6000 Frankfurt Main 1, Federal Republic of Germany*

In Spain: Please write to *Longman Penguin España, Calle San Nicolas 15, E–28013 Madrid, Spain*

In France: Please write to *Penguin Books Ltd, 39 Rue de Montmorency, F-75003, Paris, France*

In Japan: Please write to *Longman Penguin Japan Co Ltd, Yamaguchi Building, 2–12–9 Kanda Jimbocho, Chiyoda-Ku, Tokyo 101, Japan*

'She brings the malicious observation of Muriel Spark to the farcical situations of Saki . . . short, sharp and sparklingly malicious' – *Spectator*

The Sin Eater

'A first novel of startling wit and malice . . . Shamelessly clever and never vague' – *Guardian*. 'A glittering tragi-comedy of manners' – *Sunday Times*. 'There is wit, sharp perception and . . . a cutting edge of thought and words that had me grinning maliciously and guiltily' – *Daily Telegraph*

The 27th Kingdom
Shortlisted for the 1982 Booker Prize

'Alice Thomas Ellis weaves an enthralling, imaginative drama, button-holing her readers with an insistent wit and vigour . . . this new novel builds to a climax which seems the result of delighted, diabolical mischief-making' – *Observer*. 'An exquisite combination of low comedy and exalted meditation . . . her most delightful creation yet' – *Sunday Times*

The Other Side of the Fire

'Anyone who has not discovered the delights of this immensely talented novelist should certainly try her latest' – Auberon Waugh in the *Daily Mail*. 'Her prose is so consistently excellent that every other line cries out to be quoted . . . one of the wittiest writers currently at work' – *The Times*

Unexplained Laughter

A fast, wicked and devastating black comedy. 'Quite simply brilliant . . . I defy anyone to put it down unread' – Isabel Raphael in *The Times*. 'Extraordinarily compulsive reading' – *Sunday Express*

The Birds of the Air

'The forces of chaos and harmony, the isolation of human beings and their inability to understand each other's motives are presented with great poise and verbal grace . . . a bravura performance, captivating and witty' – *Spectator*

A CHOICE OF PENGUIN FICTION

A Fanatic Heart   Edna O'Brien

'A selection of twenty-nine stories (including four new ones) full of wit and feeling and savagery that prove that Edna O'Brien is one of the subtlest and most lavishly gifted writers we have' – A. Alvarez in the *Observer*

Charade   John Mortimer

'Wonderful comedy . . . an almost Firbankian melancholy . . . John Mortimer's hero is helplessly English' – *Punch*. 'What is *Charade*? Comedy? Tragedy? Mystery? It is all three and more' – *Daily Express*

Casualties   Lynne Reid Banks

'The plot grips; the prose is fast-moving and elegant; above all, the characters are wincingly, winningly human . . . if literary prizes were awarded for craftsmanship and emotional directness, *Casualties* would head the field' – *Daily Telegraph*

The Anatomy Lesson   Philip Roth

The hilarious story of Nathan Zuckerman, the famous forty-year-old writer who decides to give it all up and become a doctor – and a pornographer – instead. 'The finest, boldest and funniest piece of fiction that Philip Roth has yet produced' – *Spectator*

Gabriel's Lament   Paul Bailey

Shortlisted for the 1986 Booker Prize
'The best novel yet by one of the most careful fiction craftsmen of his generation' – *Guardian*. 'A magnificent novel, moving, eccentric and unforgettable. He has a rare feeling for language and an understanding of character which few can rival' – *Daily Telegraph*

Small Changes   Marge Piercy

In the Sixties the world seemed to be making big changes – but for many women it was the small changes that were the hardest and the most profound. *Small Changes* is Marge Piercy's explosive new novel about women fighting to make their way in a man's world.